TekLords

ALSO BY WILLIAM SHATNER

TekWar

TekLords

WILLIAM SHATNER

An Ace/Putnam Book
Published by G. P. Putnam's Sons
New York

This work is dedicated to
Marcy, Leslie, Liz and Melanie,
with a small thank-you to Grant,
and a large one to Mary Jo.

An Ace/Putnam Book
Published by G. P. Putnam's Sons
Publishers Since 1838
200 Madison Avenue
New York, NY 10016

Library of Congress Cataloging-in-Publication Data

Shatner, William.
TekLords / William Shatner.
p. cm.
Sequel to: TekWar.
"An Ace/Putnam book."
I. Title.
PS3569.H347T44 1991   90-45971CIP
813'.54—dc20
ISBN 0-399-13616-9

Printed in the United States of America
1 2 3 4 5 6 7 8 9 10

This book is printed on acid-free paper.
∞

Imagine . . . a sequel, continuity, progression

Why?   Sales, reviews, terrific
Who?   Ron Goulart—wise, witty, ingenious
        Carmen LaVia—hip, helpful and a friend
        Susan Allison, Roger Cooper and Lisa Wager—Putnam, perfect
        Ivy Fischer Stone and Fifi Oscard—also agents, also friends
And next?
Guess.

∷ 1 ∷

riday, May 16, 2120, was grey and rainfilled across most of Greater Los Angeles.

It was not going to be an especially good day for Jake Cardigan.

At a little before ten in the morning he landed his aircar on the ground-level visitors' lot next to the Oceanside Educational Academy in the Santa Monica Sector of GLA. There was a sharp wind blowing across the choppy Pacific.

The academy consisted of a series of three huge linked plastiglass domes built on pilings out over the grey, foamy ocean. Several offwhite gulls came circling down through the hard rain to settle atop the nearest dome.

Jake unbuckled his safety harness, sighed, shook his head and, with hunched shoulders, stepped out into the rainswept morning. He didn't much want to be here.

He was a sandyhaired man in his late forties, of middle height, good-looking in a weatherbeaten, worldweary sort of way. He ran from his car to the entrance of the nearest dome like someone who was still in pretty good shape.

The curved plastiglass door, which was tinted a pale blue, hissed open in anticipation.

Jake entered the large oval foyer. "I have an appointment with—"

"Halt," advised the seven-foot-tall security robot who stood, wide-legged, at the far end of the room. "Keep your hands at your sides."

Jake obliged. "As I was saying, I have an appointment with—"

"Please state your name, sir." The big robot's voice was high-pitched, a bit squeaky.

"Jake Cardigan."

"Last name first."

"Cardigan, Jake." He walked a few paces closer. "Look, I'm supposed to see the dean about my—"

"Cardigan, Jake." The gunmetal robot had three rows of tiny lights implanted across his wide chest. Several of them began flashing in sequence as he checked out Jake's name. After less than ten seconds he made a disapproving clucking sound. "You can't be admitted, I'm afraid. Please, take your leave."

Instead Jake walked right up to the security robot. "My son, Dan, is a student here—and don't blame me for that, my exwife picked out this place for him," he explained. "The dean wanted to see her this morning to talk about some problems Dan's having. Kate, though, says she can't get time off from her new job up in San Francisco and she asked me to come instead. Clear?"

"Cardigan, Jake. Convicted felon, sentenced to fifteen years in the orbiting penal colony commonly known as the Freezer," recited the big bot. "It is the opinion of the academy that convicted felons tend to have a bad influence on the developing minds of our students and, therefore, there's a rule against—"

"I was up in the Freezer," Jake cut in to admit. "However, I was released after just four years. And, as of a few weeks ago, I was given a full pardon. All the officials and toadies in our great State of Southern California, not to mention every damn official in the Greater Los Angeles government as well, now firmly believes that I was framed and wrongly sent to prison. So, unless you want to be dismantled piece by piece and donated to the nearest scrap heap, you'll let me in."

"Are you threatening me, sir?"

Jake gave a bleak grin. "I am, yeah."

"I'm designed to withstand assaults." He held up his metallic right hand, each finger of which was tipped with a different colored lightbead. "Built into this hand alone are several formidable weapons, any of which is capable of—"

"Maybe you ought to check with your bosses," suggested Jake. "Since I'm here, I'd like to keep the appointment with the dean."

After making a few rattling sounds, the robot shut its metal eyelids. Various sorts of whirrings came out of its skull and broad chest, the tiny lights flashed. "Wouldn't you know it?" he asked when he snapped his eyes open. "Our files weren't properly updated. You aren't, Mr. Cardigan, a felon at all. Allow me, therefore, to extend you a cordial welcome to the academy." He held out his left hand and a slip of yellow plazpaper eased out of one of the thin slots in his palm. "Take this pass and travel along Corridor A-2, following the green floor arrows to Door A-2/203."

"Thanks." Closing his hand on the pass, Jake stepped around the bulky robot and crossed the threshold to the corridor.

A loud hooting commenced pouring out of a row of small overhead speakers.

"Whoa there, hold it." The robot spun, grabbed out and caught Jake by the shoulder. "You ought to have informed me that you were carrying an illegal weapon."

"I'm not." Jake tapped the shoulder holster he wore under his jacket. "I have the proper permits for this stungun."

"I have to have a look at them." The robot ran his left forefinger up and down each of Jake's arms, around his torso and then, bending with a faint creak, he frisked his trouser legs. "I don't note any other weapons."

Jake took his ID packet out, flipping it open to his gun permits and his license as an operative of the Cosmos Detective Agency. "I'm a private investigator these days, with all my papers in order."

"That must be a fascinating line of work," remarked the big robot as he scanned the material with his plazeyes and his left thumb. "I bet it beats standing around in a drafty foyer all day."

"The work is usually a little more interesting than that, yeah," Jake acknowledged.

"Everything is in order, Mr. Cardigan. You can proceed."

"Much obliged." He put his IDs away and started again along the designated corridor.

•

The dean's office was large and its one seethrough wall offered a view of the rough grey Pacific. Strung out along the horizon were several robot scows. The dean's desk was made of licorice-colored plastiglass and seated behind it was a copperplated robot wearing a conservative business suit that was the same color as the rainy sky outside.

"We were expecting Mrs. Cardigan," the robot told Jake.

"I was expecting the dean." Jake lingered in the doorway.

"Dean Bushmill is, unavoidably, elsewhere. I'm the assistant dean of Oceanside," explained the dapper robot. "My name is Ticknor (M14)/SCES-30FAB."

Jake crossed the room slowly and sat down in the tin chair facing Ticknor. "My former wife couldn't get the time off to come down here from Frisco," he said. "Is Dan in some sort of trouble?"

"Serious trouble," replied the robot.

"Can you give me some specifics?"

The robot said, "Your son is currently being held in the Detention Wing in Dome #2. He is suspected of using the highly addictive electronic drug popularly known as Tek. Pending further investigation into the—"

"Wait." Jake was on his feet, frowning. "Dan's not using Tek or any other—"

"According to our records, Mr. Cardigan, there is a family history of addiction to the—"

"C'mon, Tek addiction can't be inherited." Jake, his anger growing, leaned and put both hands, palms down, on the desk. "I was a tekkie once, I've never denied it. But that was years ago and it has absolutely nothing to do with my son."

"You were also a Tek dealer, convicted and sent to prison. Growing up in such an environment would certainly influence a child toward—"

"Why the hell can't you guys keep your records up to date? I was cleared of all those charges—weeks ago," Jake told him, lifting one hand and turning it into a fist. "I just went through all this crap with your secbot."

"Perhaps I'm in error." The assistant dean robot reached to his right, touching a control pad built into his desk top. "If you'll turn your attention to the screen on the wall behind you."

A picture blossomed on the large wallscreen. A lean man of about forty was seated crosslegged in a field of high yellow grass, lecturing a scattered crowd of several hundred people. His hair was deadwhite and long, tied back with a twist of crimson ribbon. He wore a two-piece suit of silky crimson fabric. Up behind him on the sunny hillside was parked a glittering silvery landvan with the words CARA-VAN COLLEGE lettered on its side in glowing tubes of colored light.

". . . they tell you Tek will hurt you," he was saying to the seated crowd. "They manufacture stories about its being addictive, about Tek's causing epileptic seizures, about its ruining lives. Lies. All lies, my dear young friends and disciples. Tek is, if you want the truth, simply the most important discovery of our twenty-second century. Important because it has liberated the imagination, freed the mind of its fetters and, most importantly, enabled poor docile ciphers like you and like me to discover the true nature of ourselves and of our souls. Trust me when I tell you that Tek cannot at all harm you and can only liberate the . . ."

The robot had touched the panel again and the image of the sunlit field died. "I assume, considering your background, that you know who that is."

"Sure, it's Professor Joel Freedon, a nitwit who travels around the country advocating the legalization of Tek." Jake sat again. "What's he got to do with Dan?"

"We found the vidcaz you've just seen," explained Assistant Dean Ticknor, "in your son's sleep cubicle, hidden away in his property locker."

"You did, huh?" Jake stood again, walking around the desk to stand next to the robot's chair. "And Dan gave you permission to search?"

"Of course not. Our periodical random searches of the students'

1 1

belongings for subversive materials, pornography and illegal substances wouldn't be effective if we were to warn them in advance of our intention to—"

"Under the existing laws in SoCal, Ticknor, you've violated my son's civil rights," Jake told him, keeping the anger out of his voice as best he could. "On top of which, even if your search had been legal, all you've proved is that Dan has dubious taste in what he watches on his vidcaz machine. Having a copy of a lecture by a dimwit like Prof Freedon doesn't make anybody a tekkie. I'm assuming you didn't find a Brainbox or any Tek chips when you ransacked Dan's stuff."

"Well, no. The important point, however, is that he was in possession of a vidcaz that openly—"

"I think I'd better talk to the dean. Fairly soon," mentioned Jake, the bleak grin touching his face again. "Since Kate seems to think, god knows why, that this is the school Dan ought to be attending, I guess he'd best stay here for now. So I want your dean—not a robot, not an android, but somebody with a pulse—to drop all the charges and reinstate my son." He paused, taking a slow, deep breath. "Otherwise I'm going to start a lawsuit against you folks."

"Well, now." The robot raised his hand and made a calming gesture toward Jake. Then he shut his eyes. "Allow me to check up on a few things, Mr. Cardigan." His coppery skull began to produce humming sounds. Every few seconds he nodded and after nearly two minutes he opened his eyes and said, "Dean Bushmill is unable to leave the golf tournament he's playing in up at his satellite country club. He does, however, agree with you that a grave mistake has been made in the case of your son. Daniel Cardigan will be released from detention immediately and all charges erased. Dean Bushmill wasn't aware, by the way, until just now, that you were such a highly thought of member of the staff of the Cosmos Detective Agency. A very prestigious, and influential, organization here in Greater Los Angeles."

"Which proves that even deans can learn something new every once in a while."

The robot rose up. "I assume you'd like to visit with your son while you're here."

Jake hesitated a few seconds before answering. "Yeah, sure," he said finally. "I would."

▟ 2 ▙

The sound of the rain was kept out of the visitors' lounge. It hit silently at the curved seethrough walls. Jake sat alone in the large, quiet room. Down near the arched doorway a small cylindrical servomech was aimlessly polishing the nearwood flooring. The silvery mechanism wasn't functioning just exactly right and it kept bumping into the wall, backing off, polishing a small circular area, bumping into the wall again.

Jake got up, stared out at the ocean. A lone gull came diving down, skimming the churning water and plucking up something in its beak.

The servomech bumped into the wall again.

Jamming his hands into his trouser pockets, Jake started pacing. He was very uneasy about meeting with his son.

The polishing mechanism bumped into the wall, but this time it tipped over on its back.

Jake strode over to it, crouched and righted the thing. "Sounds like you're on the fritz," he said.

"Always butting in on something, aren't you?"

Jake stood and faced his son in the doorway. "How are you doing, Dan?"

Dan was leaner than Jake, an inch or so taller already, and he had the same color hair. "How the hell do you think I'm doing? Everybody here knows you're a Tekhead, so they figure I must be one, too."

"Dan, I haven't used that stuff since—"

"Okay, never mind. I'm fine, I'm great. Isn't that what you want to hear?"

"Nope, what I want to hear, first off, is what's been going on," Jake told him. "Did you really have a vidcaz of that asshole Freedon in your locker?"

"You still playing cop?"

"Did you?"

"Professor Freedon is an honest, intelligent man and, while I don't exactly agree with his views of Tek, I think he has some interesting things to say about our society."

"I just wanted to make sure the damn thing wasn't planted on you."

"Oh, yeah, that's right. People have a tendency to frame the poor Cardigans. First they framed you and shipped you up to the Freezer, now they try to get your only son shipped out of this shithole."

"Don't you like the academy?"

"I love the place, it's absolutely terrific. Is that what you came to talk about?"

Jake put his hand on his fifteen-year-old son's shoulder. "I came here because they'd tossed you in detention."

Dan jerked free of his father's touch. "If Mom could've kept the appointment, you wouldn't have come at all. So don't bullshit me."

"Maybe I wouldn't have come, Dan. The few times I've seen you since we got back from Mexico, you haven't acted especially—"

"What did you expect? You came down to Mexico and fouled up everything."

"I found the people I was hired to find—Professor Kittridge and his daughter Beth. I helped break up one of the bigger Tek cartels."

"Well, you got your reward, didn't you? I hear you're shacking up with Beth Kittridge."

Jake paused and met Dan's eye. He said quietly, "I'm seeing her, yeah."

After a moment Dan looked away. "Well, is there anything else you want to chat about? Want to see a printout of my latest grades?"

"Dan, I didn't plan to get myself sent up to the Freezer. I know I went away at a time you needed me, but—"

"Jesus, don't go trying to give me the same crap the school robotherapist hands out. Loss of the father at a crucial point in the development cycle." Dan turned away, kicking out once at the wobbly servomech.

"As for what happened down in Mexico—I didn't know at the start that your mother was tied in with any of it," Jake told his son. "And I also didn't know that Bennett Sands was going to turn out to be connected with the Tek trade."

Turning, Dan faced him again. "I'll tell you something about Bennett Sands," he said. "He wasn't, I guess, the most honest guy in the world, but he was more of a father to me than you ever were."

Jake let out his breath suddenly, shaking his head. "C'mon, Dan. Don't keep trying to hurt me just because—"

"I'm not trying to hurt you. I'm just trying to tell you the god-damn truth," his son said. "You got Bennett Sands nearly killed. Then you—"

"Listen, Dan, Sands was in cahoots with a guy named Sonny Hokori. Hokori was one of the worst Teklords going."

"Well, Bennett Sands was also looking after Mom—and me. Now she has to work that stupid job with that vidad agency up in Frisco. We owe that to you, too."

"This probably isn't a good time to debate about what went on down in Mexico," Jake said. "I had a talk with the assistant dean. They're dropping all the charges against you, reinstating you in—"

"I already know. The bot who escorted me here told me that."

"If you need anything else, call me." Jake moved toward the doorway. "I'm sorry we always—"

"I don't need you for a damn thing. You've already screwed up my life just about beyond repair," his son told him. "The best thing you can do is just stay away from me. Can you, please, do that?"

Jake stared at Dan. Finally, he nodded. "Sure."

"Why did you come back at all? Christ, I wish you'd served the whole fifteen years up in the Freezer."

Jake walked out of the room.

A few minutes later he found himself outside again on the parking lot.

The rain seemed colder and more penetrating than it had when he arrived.

∷ 3 ∷

The new Malibu supermall covered nearly five acres. Built of crystal-clear plastiglass and silvery metal, it rose up ten levels above the ground and also offered ten below-ground floors. The supermall sat just across a wide slot-roadway from the ocean.

At a few minutes after one Jake was hurrying along an AG-Level 3 walkway. He was supposed to meet Beth Kittridge for lunch in a Mexican restaurant in Ethnik Row and he was nearly ten minutes late.

Off to his left stretched Pastry Lane and as he weaved his way through the afternoon shoppers, the scents of fresh-baked cakes and pies—all piped out of an overhead bank of smell-simulator nozzles—briefly engulfed him.

He dodged a string quartet that was set up at the side of the walkway. Three humans, with a pretty blonde young woman android on cello, were playing gentle baroque music that the combined noises of the third level nearly smothered. Next came a small parade of middleaged female shoppers, each trailed by a wheeled robot shopping cart. Skirting them, Jake nearly collided with a wandering robot balladeer who was playing a popular tune from the late twentieth century. He had an enameled surface that was painted in rainbow stripes and his out-of-tune electrolute was giving off faint swirling wisps of brownish smoke. As Jake passed a boutique that specialized in Moonbase fabrics, three large gunmetal security robots came bursting out. They were dragging a veteran of the Brazil Wars, a gaunt young man still wearing the tatters of his old uniform and clutching a large handmade sign that announced—BROKE AND HUNGRY!

"No begging allowed on this level," said one of the secbots in a thick, rumbling voice.

"Jesus, I fought for you guys down in 'Zil," the onetime soldier told them. "I made it safe for you and your families. All I want now is—"

"Here." Jake handed him a five-dollar Banx note.

"Five bucks? What the hell can I buy with that?"

"Move along," another of the robots advised Jake. "No begging, no contributing to beggars."

"Five bucks," repeated the young man as he crumpled the note and stuffed it into a tattered pocket of his coat. "Have you priced any of the food in this shithole?"

Shrugging, Jake continued on his way.

On his left now was a maternity shop and on his right a hologram puppet theater.

Gathered in front of the gilded entrance to the theater were about a dozen or more small restless children. Lecturing them was a silvery female-model android in the crimson and white uniform of a supermall tour guide. "Okay," she was asking, "how many of us know what a hologram is?"

"How many of us know where the darn bathrooms are?" asked a Chinese boy.

Grinning, Jake started to circle the cluster of kids. That was when he became aware of harsh muttering directly ahead of him.

". . . no good bastard . . . kill the son of a bitch . . . Jake Cardigan . . . dirty bastard . . . kill . . ."

Lurching along the walkway, shoving shoppers out of his path, came a large welldressed, wellgroomed man in his late forties. His eyes were wide, his gait stifflegged and jerky.

Noticing him, the android guide began shooing her charges toward the opposite side of the wide walkway. "Gang, let's scoot over in front of that shop."

". . . dirty bastard . . . Jake Cardigan . . . kill him graveyard dead

. . ." Jake looked at the man. He'd never seen him before. Suddenly, the muttering man swung out and slapped one of the scattering children.

It was a small, darkhaired girl and she began to scream and sob at the same time.

Jake was caught in the swirl of panicked kids. On the crowded walkway he was afraid to draw his stungun, and he eyed the stranger warily as he approached.

". . . no good son of a bitch . . . kill him . . ." With no warning, the welldressed, wellgroomed man reached inside his coat and yanked out an electroknife. He clicked it on and the ten-inch black blade began to drone.

Jake held his ground. "Better put that away," he advised.

Instead the man lunged violently, stabbing out with the sharp, chattering blade.

Jake dodged the thrust of the knife, got in under the man's guard and elbowed him hard in the midsection.

They both went stumbling, tangled together, across the walkway and through the entry of the theater.

There were three people still inside the place, huddled up near the projection stage. One of them, a lanky teen, jumped over a row of seats and ran for a side exit. As he pushed his way out, the other two, a married couple in their thirties, went dashing along the aisle and out the same exit.

Up on the oval stage was the three-dimensional image of a lovely blonde maiden in a flowing white gown. She was about two feet high. She was tied to a stake and a ferocious emerald-green dragon was bellying toward her, snorting smoke and exhaling crackling orange flames. Rushing toward them on the back of an ebony stallion was a knight in gold armor who waved a golden sword.

Jake took all this in while he delivered several sharp punches to his assailant's ribs and struggled to keep clear of the slashes of the whirring blade.

". . . dirty no good bastard . . . better off dead . . ." He broke away from Jake, but tripped and fell onto the stage. He dropped through the image of the fiery dragon and stayed down, crouching on one knee.

"Throw away the knife, okay?"

". . . son of a bitch!" The man leaped straight for Jake.

Pivoting and dropping into a crouch, Jake avoided him. Before the disoriented assassin had regained his balance, Jake jumped forward and landed several hard chopping blows on his neck.

The man started making gagging noises. He crashed into the front row of seats, twisted around and fell to the floor.

Jake moved forward, kicking out.

His booted foot connected with the knife hand, sending the buzzing blade spinning away into the surrounding dark.

Jake grabbed hold of the man by the front of his expensive coat and tugged him upright. "Now tell me what the hell is going on."

The man's eyes suddenly snapped shut. He began to jerk convulsively, moaning. Yellowish froth came spilling across his lips. He jerked twice more, then ceased to breathe.

Jake let go of him, took a step back.

The man dropped to the floor, hitting it with both knees. He stayed that way for a swaying second or two, then fell all the way over and was dead.

Up on the stage the golden knight thrust his sword into the heart of the dragon.

■

Jake found the deadman's ID packet in an inner pocket of his suit coat. His name was Edwin L. Pland, he was an executive with a hydroponics company and lived in the Oxnard Sector of Greater Los Angeles.

Still breathing hard, Jake sank down into a front-row seat and absently started tapping the packet on his knee. "Edwin Pland. I never heard of him," he said to himself.

From behind him, an authoritative voice ordered, "Please to stand up. Drop whatever it is you're holding. Raise both hands high."

Getting up, Jake tossed the assortment of IDs down onto the corpse's chest.

Two big security robots were stomping down the center aisle, each pointing his forefinger at Jake. That was the finger that usually contained a lazgun, which indicated they had him figured for a fairly serious, and dangerous, criminal.

Lifting both hands, Jake explained, "I'm Jake Cardigan, a licensed operative with the Cosmos Detec—"

"Move away from the victim, please."

"You've got that wrong. I'm the victim or was supposed to be. This guy was—"

"You have the option of remaining silent until the law officers arrive on the scene," recited one of the secbots as he frisked Jake. "Or you can make a full confession to either of us."

"I'm the one, see, who was assaulted, so a confession isn't . . . Hey, I've got a permit for that."

The robot, having found his stungun, was easing it free of the shoulder holster. "That will be settled after the police arrive, sir."

The other security robot knelt next to the body. "Victim is dead," he announced.

Jake nodded at his stungun. "I already showed my permit to your doorman down on Level 1. Just contact him and ask him if—"

"Jake, are you all right?" It was Beth, standing at the back of the small theater.

"Yeah, I seem to have survived whatever sort of attack this was supposed to be."

"Miss," warned the robot who'd confiscated Jake's weapon, "I'll be forced to shoot you down if you take another step."

"Why would you do something like that?"

"Because you're armed."

Beth frowned at the stungun in her hand. "So I am," she admitted. "I got restless waiting at the restaurant, Jake, and decided to come hunting for you. I pulled this out when I heard the commotion in here."

"Please, miss. Surrender your weapon."

Lowering her gunhand to her side, Beth came up to the stage area. She was a slender, darkhaired young woman. "You're certain you aren't hurt, Jake?"

"Outside of a few bumps and bruises, no."

As she passed the bot, she handed him her gun, grip first. Moving close to Jake, Beth put her arms around him. "I'm glad you survived," she said softly.

"I feel pretty much that way myself." Smiling, he kissed her.

"Please stand clear of the prisoner," warned the robot.

"Why is he a prisoner?" demanded Beth.

"They think I killed this guy who was trying to kill me."

"What did kill him?"

Jake shook his head. "No idea. He just died—some kind of fit maybe."

Letting go of him, Beth went over to take a look at the deadman. "Nobody I've ever seen. Who is he, Jake?"

"I don't know."

"It's not someone you arrested back when you were a cop—a crook with a grudge against you?"

Grinning, Jake replied, "He had a grudge all right."

"Fellows, I'd like a word with you." A tall, rawboned man had come into the theater and was making his way down through the shadows to them. "I'm Agent MacQuarrie with the Federal Security Office."

Beth said, "Sorry I ran too fast for you, Hobie."

"I would've kept up if I hadn't gotten entangled with a robot gypsy violinist and several shopping carts." He showed his ID packet to the standing secbot. "I'm one of the government agents assigned to look after Miss Kittridge. I'll vouch for her and—with some reluctance—for Cardigan here."

After the robot scanned the credentials, he returned the stunguns. "Forgive us for interfering with a government operation."

"This isn't a government operation exactly," said the FSO agent, glancing over at the deadman. "He was trying to kill you, Jake?"

"So he said."

"Why?"

"No idea."

"Know him?"

"Not even casually."

"You working on a new case?"

"Between jobs."

"Something left over from your work down in Mexico a few weeks ago?"

"The Hokori cartel's defunct as far as I know. So's Hokori himself."

"Interesting. Beth, do you know this guy?"

"No. Anyway it was Jake he came after, not me."

The kneeling robot got up. "This man, based on my prelim diagnosis, was poisoned."

Jake frowned. "You sure?"

"All the indications point that way, sir. Meaning your beating of him didn't contribute to his death."

"I tend to beat anybody who comes at me waving a knife."

Beth took hold of Jake's arm. "This doesn't make much sense," she said. "Unless it is some leftover from what went on across the border."

"All the survivors," he reminded her, "are accounted for."

Just then a large black man in civilian clothes pushed into the theater by way of a side door. "Well, it's Jake Cardigan," he said as he joined the group. "Had another falling out with one of your Tek-dealing buddies, did you?"

This was Captain Hambrick of the Southern California State Police. He'd been Jake's boss once. "You know damn well," Jake told him, "that I was cleared on all those Tek charges."

"I heard about that, Jake, but it's funny—I still can't shake the notion that you're tied in with the Teklords," said the policeman. "Sooner or later—I can feel it, trust me—sooner or later I'm really going to get something on you." He bent over the corpse. "Maybe today'll be the day."

▪ 4 ▪

Jake and Beth were sitting in the shadowy last row of the small theater. The young woman, hand resting on the back of Jake's neck, was massaging gently. He was looking straight ahead, eyes narrowed.

A half dozen seats over Agent MacQuarrie was lounging in an alert way.

Up front Captain Hambrick was supervising a crew of five that included two men from his Forensic Squad and a white enameled medibot from the SoCal Coroner's Office.

"You really don't know the deadman?" Beth asked in a whisper.

"Nope."

"I don't like this. I was hoping we were through with the whole Tek business."

"No way yet of telling what prompted Pland to make a try at killing me. It could turn out he's simply a freelance loon."

"Who just ran into you here today by chance?"

"Okay, somebody had to plan this little assassination attempt," he conceded. "But that doesn't mean anybody in the Tek trade is involved. There are several—"

"Cardigan!" Up near the stage the captain was making a come-here gesture with his left hand. In his right he dangled something in a plasack.

Jake went down to his onetime boss. "Yeah?"

"Know what this is?" He held the small sack up.

In it was a silver disk, about a half inch thick and roughly two inches in diameter. There were smears of blood across one side of it. "Looks like some kind of parasite control box," he said. "I've never seen one that small, though."

"This is a variation on the sort of parasite control gadget they use in prisons in some of the less enlightened nations of the world." Hambrick swung it back and forth a few times. "Attach one to somebody and he becomes docile and obedient. This version here is a lot more sophisticated."

"Meaning it took over Pland, made him come gunning for me?"

"Exactly. You, of course, wouldn't know anything about that."

"I never heard of this kind of parasite before."

"This one is also capable, from what the Coroner's Office tells me, of delivering a fatal dose of fast-acting poison."

"That's what killed him?"

"Pretty certain it was. It can be activated from a distance. That eliminated Pland as a source of information."

"Have you checked him out?"

"Legit businessman, no criminal record. He had a couple of runins with the SoCal Revenue Service about his taxes. Outside of that, nothing," said the policeman. "He seems to have taken off from his office in the Oxnard Sector a few minutes before noon. Was supposed to meet a client over in the Westwood Sector for lunch, but he never showed up. His aircar is parked outside the supermall in Lot 13J."

Beth had come down the aisle. "May I?" She took the plasack from Hambrick, held it close to her face and studied the disk. She frowned, nodded once, handed it back. "Thanks, Captain."

"Ever seen one before?"

"Not exactly like that."

Jake asked, "Have you, Hambrick?"

"As a matter of fact, I have. This happens to be the third one we've encountered in the past few weeks," he replied. "We call the poor bastards who wear them zombies."

"Any idea who's behind them?"

"Not yet. But the other two victims of our zombies were both Tek dealers—and, unlike you, they both died."

"Did the other zombie assassins die, too?"

The captain nodded. "Yep, just as soon as they finished their chores," he said. "Odd, isn't it, that the other two targets were known Tek dealers? But you say you're completely out of that now, so—"

"I was never in it." Anger flashed in Jake's voice. "You know I was cleared of—"

"Captain, would it be okay if we left now?" asked Beth, very politely.

"Unless Cardigan would like to stay around and explain what's really going on."

Jake took a slow, deep breath. "We'll go," he said.

■

Beth had insisted on piloting his aircar. Rather than assuring her again that his tussle with the zombie hadn't done him any serious damage, he'd settled into the passenger seat.

They were flying across the afternoon toward Beth's beach condo in the Laguna Sector. The rain wasn't as heavy now, but a thick grey fog had started drifting in from the sea. The towers of Greater Los Angeles were already shrouded and most of the huge vidad billboards down below showed only as agitated blurs of color.

"From what the captain told you, this has to be tied in with the Teklords somehow—the attempt to kill you."

Jake said, "I got the impression you recognized that parasite gadget that was used to control Pland."

She concentrated on her flying. "It reminded me of something, that's all."

"Reminded you of what?"

She shrugged the shoulder nearest him. "Nothing important."

He turned in his seat, taking a look out the rear window. "Mac-Quarrie's still on our tail."

"He's okay, for a government agent. Much better than Agent Weiner on the graveyard shift. I know they mean well, but sometimes all this surveillance really annoys me."

"Your father is still, potentially, in a position to wipe out most of the Tek trade. That's why the government has to be interested in your wellbeing."

"My father," she said, bitterness in her voice. "I don't have much contact with him anymore, after Mexico. I'll never work with him again, I know that."

"Even so, you'd make the Teklords a terrific hostage."

Beth sighed. "Father hasn't even recovered from what he went through down there," she said. "Since he got back to this country he's been at that government rehab center up in NorCal. It may be months, Jake, before he's ready to finish up the work that remains to be done on his anti-Tek system. I really don't much like the idea of having all these government men lurking around for another year or more."

Jake grinned. "It does somewhat hamper my courtship."

"Is that what's been going on between us?" She laughed. "That's very quaint and oldfashioned."

"Sure, I've been courting you. Didn't I mention that?"

"No, but I suspected as much."

Jake said, "That attack on me today might have been tried because the Tek folks figure they'll have an easier time getting at you if I'm not around."

"I know that my father's convinced a slew of law officers and government agents that we were kidnapped by Sonny Hokori," Beth responded. "I was there, though, and I can't help feeling that he'd made some kind of deal and was ready to sell out to Hokori."

"I've been digging into that, Beth, but so far—"

"The point is, I'm pretty certain the Tek cartels could simply bribe Dad to delay his researches or halt them altogether," Beth said. "They wouldn't have to kill him or kidnap me."

"But that's a maxsecurity facility he's recuperating in," Jake reminded. "Be tough to get a bribe to him there."

"You've been very patient with me." Reaching over, she touched his hand. "I know I must've told you about my concerns over my father a hundred times now."

"A hundred and sixteen actually, but who's counting?"

Smiling, she asked, "Can you stop awhile at my place?"

"Not now, no," answered Jake. "There are some things I have to find out first."

∷ 5 ∷

The computer terminal chuckled. "Just kidding," it said.

Jake tapped the fingers of his left hand on the arm of his desk chair. "Anytime you feel ready to continue, Rozko."

Rozko-227N/FS was displaying a drawing of an enormous stack of papers and memos on its three-foot-square screen. "When you asked for a list of people who might still have it in for you, I couldn't help whipping up this little cartoon," it said. "Or I might have simply started running off pages of any one of the GLA vidphone directories. The overall notion being that in your years as a SoCal state cop you made considerable enemies, Jake."

"Okay, just tell me what you've got on the Hokori Tek cartel."

A picture of an ebony urn appeared on the screen. "Here you see all that remains of Sonny Hokori."

"And his whole organization is definitely out of business?"

A succession of fullcolor mugshots began to show up. "The remnants have been split up between these five gents. According to all our Cosmos sources, the Hokori cartel is no more."

Jake was sitting at his desk high up in Tower I of the Cosmos Detective Agency building in the Laguna Sector of Greater Los Angeles. He leaned forward slightly in his chair. "None of these lads has sworn to get even with me for being involved in smashing Sonny's operations?"

"Let me doublecheck." The terminal, which sat on the right side of his desk top, hummed a middle-twenty-first-century show tune, showing him a picture of a mountain lake. "Here's something soothing for you to look at while I'm digging, boss."

"Rozko, why'd they design you to be such—"

"Okay, here's the dope. There's not a single indication that any of Hokori's former business associates are planning to bump you off in revenge."

"What about friends and relatives?"

A naked blonde, lying on a floating airmattress with her buttocks thrust high, appeared next. She was smiling over her bare shoulder at whoever had taken the vidfootage. "Next three shots are of Sonny's other recent known mistresses," explained Rozko. "Interesting birthmark on the second one, huh? The whole set of them has made other arrangements, shedding nary a tear nor vowing to get even with you, the International Drug Control Agency or any of the others involved in the recent Mexican rubout of Sonny."

"Relatives?"

"None left above the ground. Sonny did have a sister—picture in a sec."

A slim, attractive young Japanese woman showed on the screen. She wore a dark pullover and slacks, was sitting in a large red wicker chair and smiling quietly.

"Here you have Frances Hokori, also known as Tora," said Rozko. "That's Japanese for Tiger. Sweetlooking lass, but had an even longer criminal record than her big brother."

"She's dead?"

"As of nearly five months ago. Killed in a maglev railroad accident just outside of Tokyo. I'll round up a pic of *her* urn in a—"

"You can forget that," Jake said. "Now check on Bennett Sands."

"Coming up," responded the terminal. "Says here he's still basking in the hoosegow, Jake. Still locked away in the Hospital Wing at the fed macsec prison up in the Walnut Creek Sector of the Bay Area. Soon as he's in good enough shape, the docs are going to fit him with a cyborg arm to replace the one you lopped off the poor bugger down in Mex—"

"I didn't do that."

"Nobody would blame you if you had, pal. The guy was making it with your missus off and on for years. He helped set you up to take that fall that landed you in the Freezer. Then the guy—"

"Has Sands had any visitors?"

"You can't have friends and wellwishers dropping in at that particular penal spa," the computer terminal pointed out. "Are you still carrying the torch for your used-to-be-wife? Just between you and me, it looks sort of fishy that she's resettled up in Frisco. In case you're fuzzy on your NorCal geography, San Francisco is just a hop, skip and a tube ride from Walnut Creek."

Jake leaned back in his chair. "Next I want whatever you can get on a couple of recent killings here in the GLA area. The zombie murders the police are calling them and—"

"Huh, here's something screwy."

"What?"

"Being faster than lightning, I started digging for info soon as the word 'zombie' popped out of your kisser."

"And?"

The screen turned deep black. "I can't tap into any of our usual sources of police information. There's a seclock on that zombie stuff, Jake."

"Can you go around it?"

"Not without an order from our Legal Department. Want I should request one?"

"Nope, I'll try some other sources first."

"Because you don't want the local coppers to know you're nosing around?"

"That's one reason, yeah."

A door panel came whispering open. A dark, curlyhaired man, about ten years younger than Jake, strode into his office. Spotting Jake, he smiled broadly. "*Amigo,* I'm glad I located you." He settled into the seat across the desk from him. "And in this most unlikely spot—here at work."

"Hi, Sid. How come you look so cheerful?"

"Can't help it, it's genetic," said Sid Gomez, Jake's partner. "As to why I'm glad I tracked you down . . ."

"A new case maybe?"

"*Sí*, and we have to get to work *muy pronto.*" Gomez popped to his feet again. "C'mon with me. We've got just about enough time to get to the funeral."

■

Gomez, as he guided the agency aircar through the rainfilled twilight, observed, "In the longago era when we were both dedicated SoCal state cops, you always struck me as an exceptionally jolly fellow. Today, though, you're nothing but gloomy."

"That's appropriate for attending a funeral, isn't it?" Jake was slouched in the passenger seat. "Whose funeral is it, by the way?"

"Don't get too emotional and tearful when I tell you, *amigo,*" cautioned his partner. "But we're enroute to Kurt Winterguild's obsequies."

Jake sat up. "That son of a bitch."

"I'm glad we decided against having you deliver his eulogy."

"I never even heard he was dead."

"For reasons bestknown to themselves, the International Drug Control Agency hasn't released the news of Winterguild's death to the media," said Gomez. "Even though he was Field Director for the whole damn Western United States."

"I don't imagine he died of natural causes."

"Apparently not. Our client is going to provide details."

"At Winterguild's funeral?"

"Bascom implied as much, when he handed me this job for us. He did pause to voice concern that you might not be able to give this investigation much enthusiasm."

"Just because I tangled with that asshole Winterguild down in Mexico, doesn't mean I can't—"

"*Sí*, I told the chief you were a dedicated pro. Sure, you decked the guy and he in turn tried to get you reinstalled up in the Freezer, but you wouldn't let that hold you back."

"What exactly is the assignment?"

"Judging from the minimum of details Bascom handed out, I'd say we have to find out who killed Winterguild."

"Hell, the IDCA will take care of that."

Gomez shook his head. "Our client is of the opinion that the drug boys are going to proceed *muy* slow on this one."

Nodding, Jake didn't say anything.

When they were near the Greater Los Angeles Spaceport, the aircar started to descend.

"You never got around," reminded Gomez while punching out a landing pattern, "to explaining the cause of your gloom."

"A combination of things. Including a visit to Dan at his school this morning."

"Are you two mending your differences?"

"Not so you'd notice."

⁑ 6 ⁑

The departing moonliner was rising up through the dusk, etching a fiery line across the growing darkness. At one edge of the GLA Spaceport sat the Eternal Rest Depot, which resembled a nineteenth-century English cottage. It had a believable slanting thatch roof, imitation wooden shutters and a profusion of ivy clinging to its stone walls. Grazing on the plazturf were five fleecy holographic sheep. Parked to the left of the undertaking parlor were three grey and black landvans.

The imitation gravel on the path between the visitors' landing lot and the cottage crunched as Jake and Gomez headed for the front door.

"Even though you didn't like him a lot," cautioned Gomez, "try not to laugh too much during the service."

The door was opened by a grim-faced robot. "Name of the deceased?"

"Winterguild." Gomez crossed the threshold.

The small foyer smelled strongly of generic flowers, and mournful music was being pumped out of hidden speakers.

The enameled robot was a gleaming black color. "You want Repose Suite 3, gentlemen," it sadly informed them. "To your left."

The suite held six rows of six seats each. There were already fifteen mourners in attendance, thirteen of them rented male and female androids in somber, suitable clothes. In the front row, head slightly bowed, sat a lean black man of about forty and in the second row was slumped a thickset blond man in his early thirties.

"Chunky guy's Nick Lefcort," said Jake, taking a back-row seat, "with the local IDCA."

Gomez settled in next to him, saying quietly, "The other guy is Gunner Gans. He's something with the Tek Division of the UN's International Security Agency."

"Not much of a turnout."

"Most folks probably share your opinion of Winterguild."

For a moment the sad music swelled up. Down the aisle from the back marched four black enameled robots. They were carrying a sealed combustible coffin. When they halted at the front of the room, one of them opened the gilded door of a lazfurnace built in the wall. The coffin was pushed into the furnace, the door shut and bolted.

Thirty seconds later a seethrough urn filled with sooty ashes came popping out of a slot just below the gilded door. The robot caught it, turned and carried the urn in both metal hands. It slow-stepped along the aisle and out of the room with the other three bots following behind.

The androids began to cry.

After approximately sixty seconds of that, they rose up one at a time and, still sniffling, filed out.

The blond drug agent left next, giving Jake a very brief nod on his way by. As Gans passed, he slowed for a few seconds to toss a small parcel in Gomez's lap. Then he was gone.

"Oof," remarked Gomez. "Hit me square in the crotch."

"What the hell is it?"

"Something, so Bascom informed me, that we're supposed to take back to the agency and take a look at." Grimacing, he got to his feet.

Jake followed his partner. "So Gans is our client?"

"Apparently so, *amigo.*"

"Couldn't he simply have delivered this package to us at Cosmos?"

"Sure, probably," admitted Gomez. "But I figure getting you to attend Winterguild's last rites made him feel good."

Jake grinned and slapped Gomez on the back. "Thanks a lot, pal," he said as they walked outside.

■

The two men were enthusiastically making love atop the floating oval airbed. One was lean and black. His partner was a muscular bald man with a single rosebud tattooed on his tanned scalp.

As they thrashed and moaned, the section of the peach-colored wall directly beyond the hovering bed started to shimmer. Then, quickly, it was glowing red.

The lovers became aware of what was happening. The black man, crying out, leaped free of the oval bed. The other sat up, went bouncing across the bed and reached toward the nightstand.

A doorway-size section of the wall turned to glowing dust and crumbled away.

Through the fresh opening stepped a plump woman, greyhaired and plainly dressed. ". . . no good bastard . . . Kurt Winterguild . . . doesn't deserve to live . . ."

The naked man was struggling to get the table drawer open. "Get the hell out of here, you old bitch!"

From her lumpy purse she took a silvery lazgun and fired haphazardly.

The bald man yanked his own lazgun out of the drawer. But before he could swing around and aim it at the wide-eyed and muttering woman, the beam of her gun sliced off his right arm just below the elbow.

He screamed a continuous scream as blood came pumping out of the severed stump.

The plump woman fired again.

This time the beam from the gun lopped off the top third of his skull.

Grimacing, muttering, the woman let her arm swing down to her side and dropped the gun. ". . . son of a bitch . . ." she said.

She started jerking convulsively, froth bubbled out over her slightly parted lips. A sudden look of puzzlement and despair flashed across her weary face before she fell to the blood-spattered floor. Someone started sobbing.

Then the picture faded from the big wallscreen.

Gomez said, "Jesus."

"Yeah," agreed Jake.

After a moment, Gomez slouched in his chair and continued, "Gans or Winterguild must have liked to record their interludes in the sack. I guess we're lucky we've got a visual ID on Winterguild's killer."

"Very efficient operation—they used a disintegrator on the bedroom wall," Jake said quietly.

His partner mused, "I'd guess the sweet old granny must have been what the cops are calling a zombie."

"She's a zombie all right." Jake stared hard at the screen.

:: 7 ::

The rain had ceased about an hour earlier. Fog was still rolling in from the sea and the surface of the chromeplated guard robot at the gateway of Beth's condo complex was misted over.

"Evening, Mr. Cardigan." It held out its right hand, palm up.

"Evening." He placed his hand flat out on the metal hand.

The guard said, "Wellsir, you've passed the first hurdle. You've sure got Jake Cardigan's fingerprints." A small panel in its chest clicked open and a jointed silver probe came snaking out. The tip rose up to take a look into Jake's left eye and then his right. "Ret patterns match. You're really Jake Cardigan."

"It's sure a relief to find that out."

The high metal gate behind the robot rattled once before swinging open. "How about this rain we've been having lately?" asked the robot, stepping aside.

"It's really something, all right."

Jake hurried up the curving ramp that led to the second level. He couldn't actually see any of the government agents who were looking after Beth, but he sensed he was under surveillance.

Beth, wearing a two-piece suitdress of Moonbase silk, let him in. She smiled, hugged him, stepped back, smiled more broadly.

He eyed her. "If I didn't know you better, I'd think you were acting . . . smug."

She shrugged, laughing. "Sit down, Jake," she invited, gesturing toward a Lucite armchair near her computer desk. "Okay, you've guessed I'm excited. I'll tell you what I've been up to—or do you want to fill me in on what you've found out first?"

Grinning, he sat down. "I don't want to risk having you explode. You tell me first."

She brushed at her dark hair and took a deep breath before perching on the edge of the sofa and facing him. "It's about these zombie murders," she began. "See, I actually had heard about those parasite control boxes before, that new smaller type. They come, as I found out this afternoon, out of Japan and have been in use around here about three months."

"Hambrick says less time than—"

"Your old police buddy doesn't know about the other three killings. And the reason for that is several government agencies are keeping it all very quiet."

Jake frowned at her. "The three other assassinations didn't have Tek dealers as victims?"

"Obviously people like Kurt Winterguild aren't Tek dealers. Nor were—"

"Hold it, Beth. How'd you find out about him? Gomez and I only just now learned that—"

"I have all sorts of friends in government agencies, remember? By spending an afternoon with my terminal and the vidphone, I was able to find out quite a lot," she told him. "My main reason for poking into this was—well, I'm concerned about you. A few weeks back I'd heard something about the zombie murders from a friend of mine. Since it looks like you're on the list of targets, I thought I'd better start asking questions."

"Winterguild and I were on the list of targets. Who else besides the Tek dealers?"

Beth said, "The first victim was a woman who was a professor at SoCal Tech. She's been with the Neobio Department for several years, but a decade ago she was doing secret government research. The—"

"How do you know about the secret stuff?"

"She used to be a friend of my father's. Now quit heckling. The second victim was a retired U.S. Army colonel. He was assassinated by a zombie down in the Baja Sector of GLA. When he was active, the colonel was attached to the West Coast Office of the Unconventional Weapons Agency. That's the same outfit the murdered professor worked for, and she was there during the same time he was."

"There could be a link between the two of them. So?"

"The killings of the Tek dealers may have been motivated by revenge or discipline. That, however, can't explain these other two."

"But you've got a theory."

"Darned right I do." She stood up, walked over to her computer desk and rested her left hip against it. "I think there are two different hit lists, two separate groups of targets. I'm anxious to find out which list you're on."

"One list could be a revenge list. What's the other one?"

She shook her head. "I'm not certain yet, but it must have something to do with some project that the professor and the colonel worked on ten years ago. It's possible that Winterguild was working on something that tied in with that, too."

"Seems unlikely to me," said Jake. "And *I* sure as hell am not involved with an unconventional weapon cooked up back in 2110 or thereabouts."

"Is there some other connection between you and Winterguild maybe, besides what happened down in Mexico?"

He answered, "This afternoon Cosmos assigned Gomez and me to investigate Winterguild's death. Our client is Gunner Gans. Know him?"

Her nose wrinkled slightly. "Met him once or twice."

Jake tapped his knee a few times. "Okay, you've got the start of a nice, clever theory maybe. It seems to me it's still pretty much on the speculative side."

"All theories start off that way."

"What you've done is stuck together some facts that may or may not be related. I still don't see the picture that you apparently—"

"Let me tell you something else I've been brooding over," she cut in. "What you're doing, Jake, you're still comparing me to the android duplicate of me you teamed up with in Mexico."

"That's not true, Beth. It's you that I—"

"Love? Didn't you first fall in love with *her*, with an android replica of me?"

"C'mon, how can somebody fall in love with a mechanism?" Leaving his chair, he crossed over to her. "I did like that other Beth, we worked well together. When she died . . . that is, when she was destroyed keeping that android kamikaze killer from doing me in, yeah, I cried. But, Beth, I knew all along she was nothing but a machine. She was also, and keep this in mind, a very close approximation of you. I didn't have to be much of a detective to figure that if the simulacrum was that bright and attractive, then the real Beth Kittridge was going to be someone special. I suppose, sure, I was like some college kid who falls in love with the image of a vidmovie actress. I was interested in you before I even found you hiding out up on Moonbase. Don't get the idea, though, that I thought more of the android than I do of you."

"That's very nice to hear. But I've still got the idea that I have to prove to you that I'm as efficient and competent as my android sim."

"I'm telling you there's no contest."

"I'm going to keep right on working on this business, whether you like it or not. Maybe I really don't have to prove anything to you, but I can prove to myself that—"

The vidphone sounded.

Stepping over to the phone alcove, Beth clicked on the screen.

Jake's exwife, looking tired and worried, appeared. "I hate to bother you, Miss Kittridge," she said evenly. "But is Jake there?"

"He is, yes."

"I have to speak to him."

Jake came over, sat facing the phone. "Kate, what's wrong? Is it Dan?"

"He's fine. Well, no, he's not exactly fine. But he's not sick and he's safe."

"I don't understand."

"Danny ran away from the academy, right after you visited him this morning. I thought they'd have notified you by now. Though if you haven't been home, you wouldn't know."

"Do you know where he is?"

"Yes, Danny's right here with me at my place in Frisco. He hopped an airbus."

"And physically he's okay?"

She nodded. "But, Jake, I do think maybe it would be a good idea for you to come up here right away. You could talk to Danny. Between the two of us we can probably persuade him to go back to school."

"Not yet, Kate. He isn't ready to listen to anything I have to say."

"Yes, I see." Kate's smile was thin. "And I imagine you're right in the middle of a new case anyway."

"Matter of fact, I am. But that's not the reason."

"Same old Jake." The screen went blank.

::8::

" 'm terribly sorry about the androids," apologized their client. "It is, unfortunately, yet another discomfort one must put up with. This is an emergency sublet, and they happen to be replicas of the owner. He's some sort of popular singer, I believe."

"Romo Styx," identified Gomez.

"Is that the fellow's name?"

"Yeah."

"He's apparently in the habit of storing the wretched things throughout the house when they're not being used to substitute for him at lesser personal appearances and the like," said Gunner Gans. "Not an especially personable young man, if one is to judge by these ungainly sims."

Jake and Gomez were meeting with Gans in the living room of his rented house in the Beverly Hills Sector. The midmorning sunlight came slanting in through the high, wide windows to illuminate the eleven lifesize Romo Styx androids that were seated and sprawled around the large, beamceilinged room. Styx was a frail youth with blond hair that was nearly white. Each mechanical replica was clothed in a tightfitting glosuit. All of them were in the inactive mode.

"First off," suggested Jake, "suppose you tell us why you don't trust the IDCA to clear up Winterguild's murder."

Gans, who was sharing a glass sofa with two dormant Romo Styx andies, sighed. "Like any other dedicated and extremely efficient man, Kurt made enemies, enemies within the agency," he explained. "Fredric Greenburr has just been appointed acting field director and, I regret to say, Freddie was not especially fond of poor Kurt. He's assured me that the murder will be solved, avenged and so on. Yet one doubts that."

"They can't afford not to solve it," Jake pointed out. "It'd be bad for business."

"*Sí*, that would make the Tek folks think agents can be killed with impunity."

Gans massaged his cheek bone. "One senses that there may well be something else involved here, some sort of cover-up."

"Why a cover-up?"

"That, Mr. Cardigan, is exactly what I'm paying the Cosmos Detective Agency such an extremely large fee to find out." He glanced up at the ceiling, left eye slowly narrowing. "The wooden beams are holograms, you know. Does that one directly above the piano seem to be fading in and out slightly?"

Gomez looked up. "Yeah, it does."

Jake asked, "In the days just before he was killed, what was Winterguild working on?"

Gans continued to stare crossly up at the flickering beam. "Considering the enormous rent I'm paying, one would expect a house in shipshape order," he complained. "What was that you asked me, Mr. Cardigan?"

"Was Winterguild working on a specific case?"

"I'm certain he was. But he and I, while we met initially because of our mutual interest in wiping out the scourge of Tek, didn't talk shop much when we were together." Gans sighed again. "One wishes now that we had. That way I might have more of an idea of what contributed to his death."

"Can you dredge up anything?" asked Gomez.

"I know that he was increasingly uneasy in the days before he was killed. My assumption is he was on the track of something important," their client told them. "He tended to become more nervous and excited in such circumstances. Poor Kurt was very boyish in some ways."

Jake turned in his chair to gaze out into the hologram foliage in the walled garden. "He mention any names, discuss any of the people involved in what he was investigating?"

"I don't really . . ." Gans sat up so suddenly he bumped his elbow on a Romo Styx. "Wait now, he did ask me if I'd ever heard of Gordon Chesterton."

"Dr. Gordon Chesterton." Jake returned his attention to the client. "He used to be a wellknown neobiologist with SoCal Tech, but he's been up in the Freezer for five or six years."

"I'd heard of Chesterton because of the notoriety when he murdered his wife," said Gans. "And because he once worked on some government projects."

"Why was Winterguild interested in him?"

Gans replied, "It had something to do with what he was investigating. Chesterton's name had come up. Forgive me, but I can't recall very much else."

Gomez inquired, "How about his informants?"

"Keep in mind that I was very much involved with my own UN work during this same period." Gans frowned up at the flickering beam. "I do have the impression that Kurt was looking forward to a meeting with someone, someone who was going to provide him with important new information."

"Did he ever have that meeting?"

"No, that awful woman burst in and . . ." He let the sentence fade, putting one hand up to rub at his forehead.

Jake asked him, "Can you maybe give us the name of at least one of his sources of information?"

The frown on Gans's forehead deepened. "The name of one of them came up in conversation, a nickname actually. Could there be a person named Subway?"

"Bingo," remarked Gomez.

Gans blinked at him. "That means something to you?"

Jake answered, "Subway is a guy who sells information to people. He usually hangs out on the fringes of the Skid Row Sector."

"Have you yourself had dealings with the man?"

"Nope, since he's also a pimp. I prefer not to use him."

"You can locate him, though, and interrogate him?"

Nodding, Jake said, "Sure, I'll have a chat with him."

"What about the Teklords?" asked Gomez. "Had there been any new threats from them?"

"One's always in potential danger from them in our line of work," answered Gans. "But I'm relatively certain Kurt hadn't heard of any new plans for revenge against him. No intended retribution for his wiping out the Hokori cartel, if that's what you mean."

After a few silent seconds Jake asked, "Why'd you pick the Cosmos Agency for this job?"

"Because you're an operative with them."

"You wanted me specifically. Why?"

"Kurt loathed you as a person, one assumes you were aware of that," said their client. "But he'd come to believe that you were, despite your stay in the Freezer, a fairly honest man and a first-rate investigator. You seemed to me, therefore, the logical person for the job of finding out who killed poor Kurt and why."

"Winterguild recommended me." Grinning, shaking his head, Jake stood. "Okay, we'll give it a try. Anything else you can tell us?"

"I'm afraid there isn't." Gans rose, too, scowling down at the two androids sprawled on the sofa. "Perhaps I can have these dreadful things stored in the basement during my stay. What's his name again?"

"Romo Styx," said Gomez.

9

The chromeplated robot waiter pointed a forefinger at Gomez's glass. Cold beer came gushing out of the metal fingertip. "Give the table your order when you're ready for lunch, gents," he said as he started away. "Enjoy."

Jake and his partner were up on the third tier of Chez Techno, a new restaurant in the Westwood Sector. The interior of the place was a blend of chromed metal catwalks and multicolor opaque plastiglass floors, walls and ceilings. There were less than ten other patrons scattered across this level.

"Joint hasn't caught on yet." Gomez sipped his beer. "I brought my current wife here for dinner the other night, though, and the food is terrific. Their chef was built in Paris."

"French robots make the best cooks." Jake was drinking mineral water.

"When our client mentioned Dr. Chesterton, you did a take that was perceptible to one with my trained eye. Know the gent, *amigo?*"

"Beth came up with some interesting stuff yesterday. It struck me that it might tie in with Chesterton." He filled his partner in on the other zombie murders and the victims' connection with a secret government project some ten years earlier.

When he finished, Gomez remarked, "If Chesterton, who also did sneaky work for the U.S. government, was involved with the same project as the deceased, we might have something."

"We might, yeah, though I'm not sure what the hell it would be, Sid."

Gomez said, after another sip of beer, "Gringo beer can never quite match *cerveza*. Are you going to dig into the Dr. Chesterton angle or shall I?"

"I'll handle it, since Beth may know something about him already." Jake rested his elbows on the small plastiglass tabletop. "Before that, though, I want to hunt up Subway."

"You think Winterguild would've been buying info from a crumbum like Sub?"

"Winterguild, meaning no offense to the dead, was a crumbum himself."

"*Es verdad,*" agreed Gomez. "Suppose I check with my contacts who know what's going on in Tek circles? Maybe I can approach the Winterguild killing from another direction, find out if the Teklords rigged that sweet granny to slice him up."

"We can meet back at the office around six tonight."

Gomez touched the button that illuminated the menu screen on his side of the table. "You and Beth are still getting along well?"

"Far as I know, why?"

"*Nada,*" said his partner. "Well, no, actually. Lately you've seemed a mite uneasy whenever you've talked about the lady."

"You are perceptive."

"It's genetic again. The Gomez clan has been eagle-eyed for untold generations. You folks having trouble?"

"Not exactly, no. But Beth pointed out something to me yesterday and maybe it's valid. She thinks I'm still in mourning over the loss of the Beth android down in Mexico."

"I can't go into anything that profound this early in the day. It sounds plausible, though."

"But that Beth was an android. I know the difference between a machine and—"

"Unfortunately, *amigo,* you can't approach everything in this world rationally. What you feel is more important than what you

think sometimes. My marriages, for example, can be used to illus-
trate the folly of mixing illusion with reality and—"

"Let's order lunch."

Gomez finished his beer. "Anything new on Dan?"

"I haven't heard from Kate since last night."

"Whatever you do, don't go up there to Frisco yet."

"I wasn't planning to."

"I've found that exwives are much more enjoyable at a safe distance. Do I have time for another beer?"

"No."

Jake, alone now, climbed up the defunct escalator steps to the
second floor of a rundown office building that sat on the edge of the
Skid Row Sector. On ascending parts of the dingy wall, interspersed
with the scrawled slurs and obscenities, were neatly lettered adver-
tisements for the man Jake was calling on. HE'S AT HOME IN THE
FUTURE—DOC NEVERS! IF IT'S WRITTEN IN THE STARS, HE CAN READ
IT—DOC NEVERS! NO PROBLEM TOO GREAT FOR—DOC NEVERS!!!

The narrow wooden door of the consulting room creaked open in
anticipation of Jake and a rusty voice croaked, "Enter and prepare
to unburden yourself of all your troubles."

The outer room was dimly lit, smelling of incense and rodents.
Jake crossed it, knocked on the door marked DOC NEVERS, ACCRED-
ITED MYSTIC.

From up near the shadowy ceiling the same rusty voice said, "The
initial fee for an illuminating visit with the fabled Doc Nevers is
. . . Jesus, is that you out there, Jake? My vidmonitor is a little fuzzy.
I thought those bastards still had you on ice up in the Freezer."

"Hey, you're supposed to know everything, Doc."

"Ah, I do, my boy. But I don't summon up specific dope unless
I'm asked for it and nobody's asked after you of late. Are you out
for good, free as a bird?"

"Yep."

The door opened. Seated in a lopsided white wicker chair in the
center of the small brown room was a chubby man of near sixty. He

had traces of grey stubble on each of his chins and was wearing a wrinkled black robe and bedroom slippers. "We'd better start off speaking of fees, Jake."

"What is it currently?" He took the only other chair, a shaky metal-legged one.

"Are you still a cop, my boy?"

"I work for the Cosmos Agency now."

"A private peeper. Shit, we all of us take a tumble from grace before it's over, huh? It's in our stars from the day we're born."

"How much for some information?"

"Since you're not a copper, it's only two hundred dollars."

Jake watched the pudgy man for several seconds. "Maybe."

"You know what the rent is on this benighted hovel?"

"I'm looking for Subway and I've been having a tough time so far."

Doc scratched at his nether chin. "Make the fee three hundred."

"Why the inflation?"

"Because it's dangerous just now, my boy, to know anything about our mutual pal Subway."

"Explain that, Doc."

"Simple. Certain rotten people are pissed off at him."

"Tek people?"

"They harbor the opinion that he shouldn't be sharing insights and snippets of news with IDCA agents."

"Agents like Winterguild?"

"That name has figured in certain of the discourses that the stars have revealed to me."

"Okay, where's Subway hiding out?"

"You might wander over into the Little Asia Sector, Jake," suggested the mystic. "Browse around the Corner Drug Store and soon a course of further action may present itself to you." He held out his plump hand.

Rising out of the rickety chair, Jake passed him $100. "The other two hundred I'll send over after I talk to Subway."

"So be it." His fingers closed on the money. "In this lousy business you learn to be a stoic."

■

The Corner Drug Store was in the middle of the block, a six-story complex sitting between the Forbidden City Automat and the Si Fan Bordello. On the walkway in front of the Drug Store's main entrance a robot in bright Oriental robes was snapping a picture of an uneasy tourist couple and a fifteen-year-old Chinese prostitute was arguing with three skysailors. Glosigns floating over the entry announced—IF IT'S A LEGAL DRUG, WE HAVE IT! THE BEST POT THAT CAN BE GOT! FREE NEEDLES WITH EVERY PURCHASE!

"Bullshit, I'm not going to do all *that* for a rotten five hundred bucks," the slim hooker was explaining to the spokesman for the skysailors as Jake pushed through the street crowd to enter the lobby of the drug emporium.

The lobby was large and circular and rose up the entire height of the building. The various shops were on tiers of balconies that circled it. On the ground level were a pot shop, a meth store, two different sinspeed outlets, a brainstim parlor, a nosepop shop and a tobacconist.

Jake made a slow circuit of the crowded lobby, glancing into shop windows, dodging tourists and more serious customers. A generic Oriental music was being played on the Drug Store's sound system, a strong teakwood incense was being pumped out of the aircirc system ducts.

"Howdy to ya, Jake." Standing beside him, smiling slyly, was a Japanese cyborg. He was lean, in his late twenties, wearing a long white synfur overcoat and a plastiglass Stetson. Instead of a right hand he had an antique silverplated sixgun.

"Howdy, Hashknife."

"Right nice to lay eyes on you again, pard."

Jake nodded, saying nothing.

"If you was to mosey into that nosepop shop yonder, you might now just find somebody who wants to palaver with you." Touching the brim of his cowboy hat with the fingers of his real hand, he went sauntering away.

"Much obliged."

The nosepop shop had a display of Snortz in its window. Above the neat stack of bright glopak containers of the product hovered a two-foot-high holographic projection of a wellknown airsoccer player. "Snortz is my favorite nose candy," the athlete was saying. "I swear to god you'll think it's real coke. Yet it's absolutely one hundred percent legal, kids!"

Jake entered the shop, causing the door to produce a short tinkling tune.

"Ever see that jerkoff play?" inquired the fat lady behind the counter.

"If you mean the jerkoff floating in your window, the answer is no."

"That dork never actually snorted Snortz in his life," she said while picking her teeth enthusiastically with her plump little finger. "Saw him go up against the Moonbase team on the vidwall the other night and he was zozzled to the gills on *real* cocaine if I'm any judge. What can I sell you?"

"I'm Jake Cardigan."

After picking her teeth for roughly another ten seconds, she said, "Damned if you aren't. Go on into the back room."

Jake went through the door and shut it behind him. The storeroom was large and along one wall were stacked plascartons of Snortz, Nosegay, Stuff and similar products. There was one small high oval window and a red sidedoor that probably led to an alley outside. There was also a glass rocking chair.

Sitting in the chair at the center of the room was a plump, smiling Chinese in a white suit. He waved cordially at Jake. "Good to see you again."

Jake took a few more steps into the room, edging to the left and nearer the red door.

The man in the glass rocker stopped smiling. "What's the matter, Jake, don't you recognize me? It's Singapore Sammy, your old pal and one of your favorite informants."

"Doc Nevers set me up, huh?"

"What are you talking about? I got some news for you about Subway."

Jake reached the door and stood with his back against it. "I only happened to find this out by chance," he said. "And I imagine your people don't know yet, since the cops have been keeping it quiet. Singapore Sammy was killed down in the Baja Sector over the weekend."

"That's a lot of crap. I'm obviously alive and well." He left the chair and it kept rocking.

"Nope, I figure you for a kamikaze android loaded with explosives." Jake turned, hit the door hard with his shoulder. It went flapping open and he dived out into the alley behind the Corner Drug Store.

He landed on the ground, rolled and stood up. He started to run for the alley mouth.

Then he noticed his escape was blocked by three blackclad cyborgs.

::10::

hey started trotting down the alley in Jake's direction. Three of them, large, wide cyborgs dressed in black and wearing pullover face masks that had narrow eye slits. The one in the lead had a black lazgun in place of his right hand.

Jake judged that the frontrunner was still about 200 yards from him. He glanced around but saw only blank walls on either side of the alley. He didn't want to go back into the storeroom where the explosive android waited.

Almost directly opposite him was a GLA Sanitation Department robot who was casually sweeping up litter and stray garbage. It was a tall, tank-chested mechanism, painted white.

Easing sideways, Jake yanked out his stungun. "Clear off, fellows," he warned the approaching trio.

The one with the black lazgun for a hand fired at him.

Anticipating the assailant's move, Jake dove to the ground, firing his stungun while he was in midair. The buzzing beam hit the first masked assassin square in the chest.

He yelped, flapped both arms, went stumbling sideways.

Meantime Jake scrambled to his feet and ran toward the sanitation robot.

Both the other cyborgs had electroknives for left hands, grey lazpistols for right hands.

The one Jake had shot slammed into an alley wall. Groaning once, he fell to the ground and stayed there.

Paying him no mind, the mechanical sweeper continued to scoop up scraps and deposit them in its open chest.

Jake fired again, but missed the dodging cyborg he'd been aiming at.

The third cyborg fired his lazpistol hand. The beam missed Jake by about two feet, but succeeded in cutting off the cylindrical head of the cleanup bot. The head, spewing circuitry, colored wires and shards of plastiglass, fell down into the robot's open chest.

"We're going to get you," called one of the blackclad assassins. "Soon now."

A smooth purring sound grew audible directly above. Jake was concentrating on the two men who were stalking him and didn't look up.

Then a sizzling beam of crimson light came slicing down slantwise. It hit the cyborg who'd taunted Jake, cutting him neatly in half at the waist.

When the remaining assassin saw the two chunks of his associate slap to the ground, splashing blood and innards, he yelled, "Holy shit!" Spinning on his heel, shaking violently, he started to run.

Going by on the street beyond the alley mouth was one of the hourly dragons and fireworks parades that the Little Asia Chamber of Commerce staged for visitors. A long scarlet, black and gold robot dragon was writhing and lurching past, breathing out long sparkling streamers of fire. Firecrackers exploded all around it.

The running cyborg had to halt at the edge of the passing parade. The beam from above came crackling down again and caught him.

It lopped off his head, hood and all. The head went spinning away, bouncing down on the street directly in the path of the zigzagging dragon.

"Jeez, it's a good thing I got here when I did," remarked an amplified voice from above.

Jake, stungun still in hand, looked up at the rainbow-hued aircar that was dropping down for an alley landing.

Piloting the multicolored vehicle was a demure-seeming teenage girl dressed in the green shirt and tan jumper that was the uniform of a very exclusive private school in the Bel Air Sector. The car settled down near him and the passenger-side door popped open. The darkhaired girl leaned and smiled across at him. "I don't think you could've saved your ass without my intervention, Jake."

"Playing hooky today, MariAlice?"

"Zish. Is that the thanks I get for pulling your nuts out of the fire?"

He told her, "I think I was winning the contest on my own and if—"

"Congratulations on surviving, Jake." Singapore Sammy had stepped into the alley and was coming toward him with his right hand held out. "Let me shake your hand."

Jake hopped into the passenger seat. "Take this thing up."

"Somebody you're avoiding?"

"Think he's a kamikaze."

"Zish!" She whapped the control panel with one small fist.

The rainbow aircar shuddered once, then shot straight up into the afternoon.

"Is that any way to treat a pal?" shouted Sammy, jumping, shaking a fist.

When the aircar was 200 feet up, MariAlice put it on hover. "Might as well defuse that schlep." She flipped a toggle.

A beam of intense green light shot down out of the belly of the aircar. At the same time the car started to climb higher.

Five seconds after the beam touched Sammy he exploded with an enormous whumping boom. He was scattered all across the alley, the white suit shredded into thousands of pieces of flickering cloth confetti, his wiring, circuitry and tubes spinning in several directions and then slamming into the alley walls. Smoke, dark and thick, came climbing up from the spot where he'd been standing.

"Your hunch about him was right," said the girl, giggling. "That was sure a kamikaze, Jake."

"He blew a big chunk out of the back wall of the Drug Store."

"Serves them right, doesn't it, for sicking the bastard on you?"
Jake said, "I guess it does at that. What were you doing here-abouts?"

"I didn't come of my own free will. And I don't much like rescuing doddering old cops." She punched out a flight pattern.

"I'm a doddering old private detective these days, child."

"That's right, I forgot. Same thing," she said as the aircar swung southward. "My uncle wants to meet with you."

Jake shook his head. "Not just now, MariAlice. I'm working."

"He knows you're working. That's what he wants to see you for. Catch?"

"Okay, I'll accept the invitation." He grinned and settled back into the passenger seat.

■

The Dinelli estate was underwater. Protected by a vast, watertight plastiglass dome, it covered three acres off the coast of the Malibu Sector. Leo Dinelli was sitting with Jake on the terrace that over-looked the tennis court. He was a tall, slender man, greying, and he controlled the Mafia in SoCal.

There were globes of white light floating at various spots, but the sunlight that came down through the water dominated and gave everything a pale blue-green tint.

On the tennis court two pretty blonde young women were play-ing. "Androids," explained Dinelli, noticing Jake's glance.

"You can tell the andies from Uncle Leo's human girlfriends," said MariAlice, who was sitting, legs crossed, on the stone railing that circled most of the flagstone terrace, "because they're over twice as smart."

"Go do your homework."

"Did it."

"Then sit quietly, be a nice girl, don't interrupt."

"Zish."

Jake asked, "What did you want to see me about, Leo?"

"You've never thought much of me, Jake."

"If he's like most people," put in MariAlice, "he loathes and—"

"Go away," suggested her uncle.

"Okay, sorry. I'll be as silent as one of your mistresses." She clapped a hand over her mouth, winking at Jake.

"I was a cop when I first met you," Jake reminded him. "That automatically made us opponents."

"Yeah, but right now we have the same enemies—the Teklords."

"True, but that's not a hell of a good basis for a friendship, Leo."

Dinelli leaned forward, resting his hands on his knees. "You know we've been putting a lot of money into developing Koke," he said. "To our way of thinking—and market research tends to back this up, Jake—Koke is the best synthetic drug available today."

"Yeah, but it's still illegal."

"True," admitted the Mafia chief. "Our biggest problem is that Tek continues to outsell us in every new sales region we enter. My brother Gig still insists Tek is just a fad that'll fade away, but I don't agree. Still, with Koke I think we've finally got a product that makes a good addition to the more traditional hard drugs the Mafia is noted for distributing."

"If you'd ever bother to watch those Prof Freedon vidtapes I loaned you, Uncle Leo, you'd realize that there's more to Tek than simply getting high or—"

"Jake, you did a damn good job against Hokori down in Mexico. Anything further you can do to help smash the Tek cartels would be—"

"Anything I do won't be so you guys can then move in and peddle Koke, Leo."

"Hey, I'm not asking you to endorse our product." Dinelli looked again at the tennis game. "Although of all the so-called dangerous drugs, Koke is the safest. If we could only legally advertise the stuff, explain to the public that here they have a product which—"

"Is this all you wanted to talk about?"

"No, I got a couple of other things." He left his chair, went over to lean against the railing. He seemed to turn a deep shade of blue for a moment as the fluctuating light from above touched him. "Jake, we've been picking up reports that the Tek bastards have put out orders to have you killed off."

"I already suspected that. Do you know why they're gunning for me?"

"All we know so far is that they want you put out of the way as quick as possible."

"Does it have something to do with what happened to Sonny?"

"Not sure, but it looks like the orders came out of Japan."

"From who?"

Dinelli gave a negative shake of his head and returned to his chair. He leaned back and gazed up at the brightly colored fish that seemed to be flying by above. "Can't answer that one yet, Jake."

"What about Winterguild?"

"That son of a bitch. I never got along with him."

"Did the order to kill him come from the same people who want me extinct—or did you folks have him taken care of?"

"Naw, we don't operate that way, Jake. Rubbing out government agents is unlucky," said Dinelli. "All we know about the Winterguild kill is that he was getting too close to something big the Teklords have in the works."

"Something new they're planning?"

"That's what we suspect. Have *you* heard anything about it?"

"Nope."

"When you find out, let me know."

"C'mon, Leo. I work for the Cosmos Agency. Anything I find out, I pass along to our client."

"I could arrange to see that you were paid, say, an honorarium. Something around $250,000 for just keeping us in the loop."

"Zish, uncle. Don't you realize yet that you can't bribe Jake?"

"An honorarium isn't a bribe. Go feed your dog."

"I already did. He's eight pounds overweight as it is."

Jake stood. "I have to be moving along, Leo."

"I appreciate your taking the time." He rose. "I can, with no trouble at all, put some of my people to looking after you. From what MariAlice was saying, you can use a little extra protection these days."

"No, thanks."

MariAlice hopped down off the railing. "I'll run you back to your office, Jake," she volunteered.

Her uncle inquired, "Don't you have studying to do?"

"All done."

"Okay, but don't go insulting Jake. And absolutely no stunt flying." He held out his hand.

Jake hesitated a few seconds, then shook it.

▐▌ 11 ▐▌

He heard the brawl before he saw it.

Jake had landed his aircar on the ground-level lot below the Beachtown area of the Santa Monica Sector. He was due to rendezvous with Gomez here in about ten minutes. While he was walking across a yellow stretch of simulated sand toward the ramp leading up to the boardwalk, he started hearing considerable raucous noise from up above.

"Oof," cried somebody.

Next came the sound that an electropiano might make falling over, followed by gasps and groans and the noise of various breakable building materials being smashed and shattered.

Operating on the hunch that this could have something to do with his partner, Jake went running up the ramp. The curving plastiglass boardwalk paralleled the curve of the beach and as Jake reached it something that was probably the detached left arm of a chromeplated robot came flying straight at him.

He ducked to avoid it and ran along the boardwalk in the direction of the commotion. On his right stretched the quiet Pacific Ocean, on his left a collection of Beachtown business enterprises—TORTURE GARDEN MOTEL, KEEN TEEN CANTEEN—NO HOOKER OVER 16, INTERNATIONAL LOTTERY PARLOR, COMMITTEE TO LEGALIZE TEK HEADQUARTERS, THE BODY ELECTRIC BORDELLO—BEST ANDROID HOOKERS IN GLA!! MA DREAM'S SALOON.

The saloon, which was where Gomez was going to meet him, was the point of origin for the brawl. Part of the fracas had spilled out onto the boardwalk. A one-armed robot, who was probably the bouncer, lay sprawled at the bottom of an agitated heap that included another, tackier robot, three burly skysailors in full uniform and a snarling robot dog painted a bright green.

Skirting the pile of struggling men and mechanisms, Jake eased around the remains of a white electropiano that had collapsed right on the threshold, and pushed through the yellow plaswood swinging doors.

The brawl was continuing on the inside. The place was built to resemble an early twentieth-century saloon. It had a long ebony bar with a glittering brass rail, darkwood booths and a substantial free-lunch counter. At the moment the android piano player, his authentic derby pulled far down over his plastic ears, was stretched out beneath the long lunch table, not functioning, and garnished profusely with salad and condiments. Six or seven husky human patrons were enthusiastically pummeling and booting each other all around the sprawled andy. A green robot dog much like the one on the stack outside was biting the fat ankle of an obese blonde woman who Jake was fairly certain must be Ma Dream herself.

At one of the booths Gomez was disentangling himself from a table, wiping his skinned knuckles gingerly across his chin and shaking his head forlornly. A skysailor was slumped unconscious on the far side of the lopsided booth.

Noticing his partner, Gomez smiled and waved. He made his way over to Jake. "I assure you, *amigo,*" he told Jake, "that I had nothing to do with precipitating this shindig."

"Well, it was probably good exercise for you."

"So help me, I was about to pay a call on my final informant of the day—who happens to reside in the bowels of this rowdy bistro— when a disagreement arose among some skysailors as to the relative merits of a pair of gaudy robodogs. I've always favored robocats myself."

"Can we . . . oops." A husky skysailor had come lunging over to try to take a poke at Jake. Jake avoided the flung punch, caught the big man's arm and used it as a lever to toss him across the room. The skysailor smacked squarely into Ma Dream and the growling green dog, knocking them apart. "As I was saying, Sid, can we both call on your contact?"

"*Por supuesto,* sure." Blowing at his knuckles and wincing, Gomez nodded. "It's Joe Waterloo—you know him, don't you?"

"Better even than I want to, yeah."

"There's a hidden entrance back near the gents." Gomez led the way. *"Vamos."*

∙

They made their way along a chill, twisting underground corridor. Off somewhere unseen water was dripping loudly.

"I sure hope," mentioned Gomez, "that that sound isn't the vast Pacific getting ready to bust into this tunnel."

Jake grinned. "What have you been finding out?"

"Before I answer that," said his partner, "tell me what you've been indulging in. Even in this dim light I can see that you've been in some sort of fracas yourself."

"Matter of fact, I was." Jake gave him a quick account of his day up to that point.

At the corridor's end was a narrow arched doorway, partially covered with a screen of dangling beads.

"Joe?" called Gomez.

"I still haven't succeeded in my chief labor, Gomez—if that's what you dropped by to inquire about."

"I do have some inquiries, but not about your prime project." He parted the strings of beads and allowed Jake to precede him into a vast cluttered workshop. "I brought my colleague along with me."

Initially it looked as though several naked young women were lying about on the worktables. But they were actually only androids.

Joe Waterloo was a heavyset man in his middle thirties, moustached and balding. He had on a frayed blue smock, was holding a soldergun and slowly circling a table on which was outstretched a naked female android face up. He ignored Jake and talked at Gomez. "They seem to wear out faster than ever these days and need more frequent repairs," he said. "This particular hooker is from Vegas II. What part do you think wears out first?"

Gomez said, "Joe, the answer is obvious."

"It isn't, Gomez, because actually the ears go first. You know why? Because half of the nitwit customers just talk to them. They pay their fee and then they tell these mechanical bimbos their problems, their secret sorrows, their dimwit hopes and dreams. Blab, especially incessant blab uttered close to the delicate hearing mechanisms, futzes them all up. Nobody wants a deaf whore."

Jake folded his arms and leaned against the wall.

Gomez said, "I'm in need of some information, Joe. I trust you still have your sideline."

"You know what my greatest problem is?"

"Tell me."

"All I have in this world is sidelines. I repair android hookers for the Mob, I provide hard-to-get info for a select list of clients, I repair appliances and servos for my friends—of which I have, bless Bess, precious few. Do you think that's why we were put on Earth?"

"Yes, I do, José. As I see it, in your case at least, providing information to others is a sacred calling. Now, what I need to know about is—"

"I've got to tell you, Gomez, that I'm really close to success with my major project, my magnum opus as it were."

"Wouldn't it be better—and I've mentioned this before—if you left this cavern and found a real human ladyfriend? Building one of your own, seems to me, is too much like the repair work you do all the time on these—"

"I'm not building myself a floozie." When Waterloo scowled, his moustache rose and fell. "I am building, keep in mind, my ideal woman. She's based in part on Doris Dinkins, my childhood sweetheart. I say, in part, because I—"

"Couldn't you simply go out and hunt up this Doris Dinkins? Be a lot simpler than starting from scratch and risking—"

"The real Doris Dinkins despises me and has for years. Besides which, she's a flabby matron of thirty-six now and lives with her halfwit husband and three halfwit children out in the San Berdoo Sector. No, my android creation will be a lot better than her."

"Well, I'm here to help finance your great work. I stand ready to pay you the usual fee for information."

"The price has gone up." Waterloo set his soldergun down near the bare foot of the damaged android hooker. He looked over at Jake. "What do you think, Cardigan?"

"About what?"

"I understand you were shacking up with a very high-class android down in Mexico. Then you replaced her with the real dame she was based on. What I'd like to know is—"

"Joe," cut in Gomez, grabbing hold of the fat man's arm, "we came here to talk business. Not to speculate—"

"I'll bet you," said Waterloo, "I'll bet you, Cardigan, that you got along a hell of a lot better with the android. Real women, see, they can't help but have quirks and mannerisms that'll annoy you sooner or later. Take Doris. She was—"

"How high have you raised your prices?" asked Gomez.

"Twenty-five percent," answered Waterloo, turning away from Jake. "The cost of everything is going up."

Pushing the long legs of the blonde android slightly to one side, Gomez perched on the edge of the worktable. "I'm interested in the recent bumping off of Kurt Winterguild."

Picking up his soldergun again, Waterloo shook his head. "You better go carefully on this one."

"Okay, what have you heard?"

"Bits and pieces. I'll have to charge you two hundred dollars."

"A deal. *Habla.*"

Waterloo said, "A consortium of Teklords has got something new and big in the works. Winterguild was engaged in trying to gather details."

"What are they planning?"

"That part I don't know."

"Can you find out?"

"Nope, nossir, no. Not if I wish to remain among the living."

"Is that why Winterguild was knocked off?"

"Not exactly, Gomez. It's more complicated, as I understand the setup. Winterguild was working to find out what they're planning—

but the guy was also trying to run down somebody they didn't want him ever to get near."

Jake asked, "Would that somebody have any connection with Dr. Gordon Chesterton?"

"I don't know," answered Waterloo, still looking at Gomez. "But I've never heard of Chesterton."

Gomez asked, "What cartels have teamed up?"

"I'm not aware of that, either. However, I do know something that'll help you find out," said Waterloo. "And if you do the nosing around instead of me, Gomez, there's much less likelihood of my getting put to rest before my great work is completed."

"Tell me then."

"Tomorrow, so I hear anyway, there's going to be a very important meeting."

"Of the Teklords involved?"

"That's it exactly."

"Okay, so where are they gathering?"

Waterloo pointed ceilingward with the barrel of his soldergun. "You know where The Casino is, don't you?"

"*Sí*, it's an orbiting gambling joint—a flying tourist trap. Is that going to be the setting for this get-together?"

Waterloo nodded. "I'll throw in some free advice," he said. "If you do go up there, Gomez, be goddamn careful."

" 'Be goddamn careful' happens to be one of my family mottos," Gomez assured him.

Jake asked, "Any of the Japanese cartels tied in with this meet?"

"Don't know." Waterloo gave an impatient cough. "I got two more of these floozies to patch up before I can even go to lunch, Gomez. I don't have anything more to tell you."

Gomez handed him some folded Banx notes. "*Gracias* then, Joe."

Jake went into the corridor first, his partner following.

Gomez whistled a few bars of a Mexican folk song as they walked. Then he said, "His queries about Beth looked like they upset you, *amigo.*"

After a few seconds Jake replied, "I guess they did."

:: 12 ::

alt Bascom's office in Tower II of the Cosmos Detective Agency building was large and cluttered. The agency chief himself was small, compact and rumpled. He was sitting now, one leg dangling, on the edge of his wide Lucite desk. He was staring up at the ceiling and scratching at his close-cropped grey hair. "The Winterguild bumpoff," he said, "starts to look suspiciously like part of something bigger."

Jake was in a canvas chair near the hologram projection screen. Gomez was sharing an aluminum armchair with several fat bundles of faxmemos.

Gomez said, "It's almost certain the major Tek cartels have something afoot, boss."

"As yet we don't have sufficient details," observed the agency chief.

"*Es verdad.*"

Bascom quit contemplating the distant ceiling and frowned at his two operatives. "If what the Teklords are up to is of sufficient importance, we ought to be able to earn considerable government gratitude if we come up with some answers ahead of them," he said thoughtfully. "Cosmos can always use more gratitude, and I can usually parlay that into lucrative assignments. There might even be the possibility of financial rewards on the side."

"So we keep working on the Tek angle," said Jake, "as well as Winterguild's murder?"

"Sure, because that's not going to hurt our client and it's bound to do us some good," answered Bascom. "One of you lads should keep digging here in GLA, while the other gets his ass up to The Casino. You can catch a shuttle out tonight, in fact, and arrive there ahead of the scheduled Tek meeting."

Gomez glanced over at his partner. "Since I'm fonder of games of chance, *amigo,* I volunteer to make the jaunt."

"I'd rather stay here just now. And this way I can concentrate on tracking down Doc Nevers."

"I take it," said Bascom, "that our mystic stoolie has vacated his usual place of business."

"Right after he sent me over to meet that kamikaze."

"It will be illuminating when you find out who paid him for that little task."

Gomez said, "Kamikazes, zombies. These louts are sparing no expense when it comes to wiping you out, Jake."

"It's flattering."

The agency chief said, "We also have to find out more about this Dr. Chesterton, and those two scientists who recently went on to glory."

"I'll take care of that," said Jake.

"We got in a case this morning, Sid, that you can probably use as a cover." Bascom searched his desktop clutter for a while, then gave up. "I'll get you the paperwork before you take off tonight. You've heard of Victoria Dorado, haven't you?"

"The madcap heiress to the vast SoyFoods fortune."

"The same. Victoria is twenty, blonde at the moment. Seems she's run off with yet another undesirable fortune hunter. Her guardian has hired us to find her and persuade her to come back home."

"Vicky is, as I recall from browsing through her dossier once, fond of gambling."

Nodding, Bascom said, "That means The Casino is a likely place to search for her. You can go up there openly as a Cosmos op, Sid.

Tell the goons who operate the place that you're working on the Dorado case. Matter of fact, you might as well see if the nitwit is holed up there."

"Okay if I depart now?" Gomez stretched up out of his chair. "I'd like to see my current wife at least briefly before I blast off for that gambling hell."

"Anything else you have to bring up, Jake?"

"Nothing, no." He stood, too.

"All right, good luck, gents, and try not to get killed," said Bascom. "If you do get knocked off, try to see that it doesn't cost the agency anything."

■

Jake followed Beth into her kitchen. "Is it okay if I don't answer your question?"

"All I asked was how things went today." She sat on an orange stool, watching him. "Wrong line of inquiry, huh?"

Grinning, he replied, "Okay, I may as well tell you."

"I think I can guess. They tried to kill you again, didn't they?"

He took a chair at the bright yellow table. "Well, yes. With a kamikaze android this time."

"Jake." She came over, stood behind him and put her hands on his shoulders. "Please tell me about it, all the details."

Reaching up, he put his hand over hers. He then recounted what had happened over in Little Asia. "As yet nobody seems to know why," he finished. "But it's pretty definitely the Teklords who're behind it."

"It must tie in with the other killings."

"Ever hear of Gordon Chesterton?"

"Of course." She took her hands from his shoulders and went around to sit opposite him at the round table. "Chesterton worked on the same project with Dr. Mildred Rhodie. She's the woman I told you was murdered by one of the zombies. Colonel Robert Keazby, the other victim, was also involved with that project."

"What were they working on?"

"My father was quite upset about it at the time, so we discussed it quite a lot," she answered. "Chesterton's a neobiologist, same as Dr. Rhodie. He'd persuaded some important people in the government to allow him to work on a new synthetic plague virus. An extremely efficient and virulent one, from what my father was able to learn. As you know, Jake, the United States has fluctuated over the past decade on whether or not to allow this sort of research to be undertaken at all. Technically, biological weapons of the sort Chesterton was developing haven't been legal since all the trouble over their use in the last Brazil War. But the official policy at that time, ten or so years ago, wasn't exactly crystal clear, so he was able to get a go-ahead. That's why my father—who still seemed to have some moral sense back then—became so upset. He protested to several government officials, formed committees, agitated to get Chesterton's project halted."

"That do any good?"

"I was never certain," she answered. "There was a great deal of circumlocution, everything just dragged. Then Chesterton killed his wife and while his trial was going on the project was, very quietly, shut down. Far as I know, it's currently against even clandestine U.S. policy to work on a biological weapon of that sort."

"Chesterton had several years to work on his plague virus—did he perfect it before the project was shelved?"

"I don't think so, but I can try to find out for sure."

"Yeah, you'd better do that."

Beth leaned back in her chair. "You remember the murder case, don't you?"

"Yeah, I was still with the SoCal State Police then. It happened not too long before . . . before I was sent up to the Freezer."

"I'm sorry, Jake. I know you don't like to talk about that. I shouldn't have mentioned it."

"Eventually I'm going to have to discuss it. Being in suspended animation for four years, stuck away in a cell the size and shape of a coffin, that makes an impression on you." He laughed quietly, stood up to walk over to the window. The night was starting to close in outside. "Chesterton's doing fifty years. They say you're not supposed to feel anything while you're in that state, that it's no worse than a short nap. But . . ."

"The worst part must be waking up, coming back home after fifty years. You haven't aged at all, but everyone else you know—wife, children, friends—they've gone on without you. They're older now, much, much older, or dead and gone."

"Even being shut away for only four years can be damn unsettling."

"*Only* four years? That can be a very long time, too." She reached across the table to take hold of his hand.

"It was for me, yeah. Things changed a lot—and the worst part of it is that I wasn't around when Dan needed me." Jake turned his hand in hers, squeezed. "I just can't get him to realize that I didn't have any choice. You'd think a cop's son would understand. When they arrest you, try you and sentence you, you don't have any say. You just go serve your sentence."

Beth, slowly, let go of his hand. Standing, she came around to his side of the table. "There's something else I want to talk about."

He took hold of her around the waist. "Seems like all we do when we're together is talk."

"When I was angry at you, I said some things about you and the android—"

"Could be you're right." He, very gently, pulled her down onto his lap.

"What I never got around to saying was the most important thing," she told him. "We came to know each other in a pretty odd and unusual way, a special way. You knew the Beth simulacrum before you knew me. You liked her and so when you met me, you liked me, too."

"Like isn't anywhere near a strong enough word, Beth."

"Don't interrupt, just listen, Jake. You still don't seem to have accepted the fact that it was *me*—the, far as I know, authentic and original Beth Kittridge—who made the choice to fall in love with you."

"I know." He kissed her.

Putting her arms tight around him, she kissed him back.

The vidphone sounded.

It sounded again.

Reluctantly, Beth rose and crossed to the kitchen phone alcove. "Yes?"

"Is my father there?" It was Dan on the phonescreen, looking unhappy and concerned.

Jake hurried over to take the call. "Is something wrong, Dan?"

"I've been trying to find you all over," his son said. "Then I thought you might be there."

"You look very upset. What is it?"

His son said, "You don't have to do anything about this if you don't want to, but I thought I'd better call you. Mom's sick."

"What do you mean—is she with you now?"

"No, she's very ill . . . she's in the hospital. It's serious, real serious . . . and they . . . I don't know, Dad. She's maybe going to die."

"What is it—what's wrong with her?"

"Nobody's sure yet. The doctors think maybe a virus . . . it came on very sudden. Started this afternoon and within a couple of hours . . . I figured I should phone you even though you aren't actually married any longer, but . . ."

"I'll be up there soon as I can tonight. Where is she?"

"The Marina Hospital here in Frisco, Dad. I'm calling from there now. They've got her in the Isolation Wing, but I'm out in the Reception Area because they won't let you inside. That's where I'll be. You can't see her up close, but—"

"That's all right, I can be with you and that's important, too," Jake said. "I'll be there within two or three hours."

"If you're too busy—"

"Two or three hours, Dan. You try to take it easy." He hung up. Beth said, "A virus."

"Just a coincidence," he said. "Okay, I'll call Bascom and tell him I'm going to take a day off from the Winterguild case."

"I'll come along with you to San Francisco."

"Good, I'd like to have you with me."

She asked, "You're not doing this just for Kate, are you?"

"My relationship with her was actually over and done before I even went up to the Freezer," said Jake, standing. "Thing is, I didn't know it then. Didn't know it until I got out."

"You're mostly doing this so you can be with your son."

"Maybe I can help him get through this, maybe I can still salvage something."

::13::

omez decided to ignore the stripper.

She was a foot-high blonde holographic projection doing her act in the exact center of his table in the shuttle cocktail lounge.

There was a control panel at the edge of the small square black table. Gomez had touched the NO ENTERTAINMENT key twice, but the blonde wouldn't go away. He'd also tried the STRING QUARTET and the DIRTY WRESTLING keys, but the stripper remained and continued to shed her clothes.

"On the fritz," he concluded, picking up his glass of beer and glancing casually around.

There were about forty tables in this particular lounge, which was one of three onboard the Casino-bound ship. There were about seventy patrons crowded into the room and at least half of the tables had the stripper stripping.

Behind the silverplated bar roamed two large goldplated robot bartenders and circulating through the dimlit lounge were three beautiful blonde barmaids. They were androids, identical in looks and sparse costumes.

Gomez recognized a few professional gamblers in the crowd and one wellknown pimp. But he didn't spot anyone he'd ever encountered in the line of duty or whose picture he'd come across.

That might mean that nobody had spotted him either. His cover story was a mite risky to bring off, since he had to pose, not as somebody else, but as himself working on a spurious case.

He sipped his beer.

The shuttle had departed from the GLA Spaceport a little over an hour ago and Gomez had, casually and unobtrusively, already checked out the other two cocktail bars. He'd come across nobody suspicious there either.

Setting his glass down, he gave the control panel another try. The stripper didn't go away, but two greased wrestlers joined her.

"Perhaps our technological society isn't as perfect as I've been led to believe," he said to himself.

Three tables over a plump tourist with a full red beard suddenly fell clean off his chair. Hitting the plastiglass floor with a rubbery thump, he started laughing.

Close to Gomez's right ear someone said, "Well, why's a top Cosmos operative heading up to The Casino—are you planning to crash the Teklords' meeting?"

■

Dan came running across the Reception Area to Jake.

Jake held out both arms to his son.

The young man pulled up a few feet short of him, out of reach of an embrace. "Where's your girlfriend?"

"Waiting downstairs. Any news?"

The fifteen-year-old's shoulders slumped, he shook his head forlornly. "Nothing, Dad. They just keep giving me the same old bullshit," he answered. "Maybe you can get them to tell you . . . I'm afraid . . . she's going to die or something."

"I'll find out what's going on, Dan."

The Reception Area for the Isolation Wing was large, grey and white in color. One wall was a oneway seethrough plastiglass, looking out on the dark night San Francisco Bay and a scatter of brightlit floating restaurants. Two walls contained rows of cubicles and in each was a patient monitor screen.

Dan gestured at the monitors. "We can go look at her, if you'd like. On one of those screens over there."

"Yeah, let's." He followed the young man to an empty cubicle.

Dan touched the keyboard beneath the three-foot-square view-screen. "Mom's in Room #134," he said. "She doesn't look . . . she looks really bad."

Jake's exwife appeared on the screen. She was lying on her back in a narrow floating airbed, covered to the waist with a thin white plassheet. Her face was deeply flushed, perspiring. Her eyes were closed, underscored with dark shadows. A white enameled medibot was in the process of administering a shot with a needlegun that was attached to its wrist.

Dangling down from above was an intricate tangle of colored wires and tubes, all attached to Kate's body, sticking into her arms, her side, her throat. Breathing gear was attached to her chest, a plasmask covered her nose and mouth.

Jake watched the sad image on the screen.

Dan said, "All those things sticking into her, they must hurt."

"It's standard procedure." He put his hand on his son's shoulder, squeezed. The boy didn't move away. "Can I talk to her doctor?"

"All you can do is hit a number and talk with a hospital andy. Her real doctor is named Habib, but I only saw him once, just after she was brought in. That was really rough, Dad. It took a hell of a long time for the skyambulance to get to the apartment . . . waiting for it and then trying to explain what was wrong. . . . She was unconscious by the time they finally got there. I don't know, maybe if I'd acted faster—"

"Sounds like you did fine, Dan. Don't blame yourself for the way the hospital handles things."

"It's just that I . . . you know, I don't want Mom to die." He moved clear of Jake's hand, lowered his head and turned his back to the screen. He pressed his lips tight together, hesitating on the edge of crying.

"How do we go about talking to somebody?"

Dan sniffled once, wiped at his nose. "Here, I'll do it," he offered, turning to the keyboard again. "You just have to hit MD and then 134."

Kate's image popped off the screen, replaced by a picture of an empty white desk.

After about ten seconds a very handsome blond man in a white medical jacket hurried into the scene, seated himself at the desk and smiled. "I'm Dr. Redfield. How can I help you? Oh, and I'm required by NorCal State law to inform you that I'm an android practitioner, not a human." He tapped the tag on his jacket pocket with his forefinger. It read AND-MD.

"Jake Cardigan. I'd like a report on the condition of my former wife, Kate Cardigan."

"That would be Kathleen McRobb Cardigan you're inquiring after, sir?"

"Christ," muttered Dan, "I already told this asshole all this."

"That's her, yes," said Jake. "Can you tell me exactly what it is she's—"

"Mrs. Cardigan was admitted at 4:45 P.M. this afternoon."

"What's she suffering from?"

"Her condition is serious. We're doing the best we can. Because of the nature of Mrs. Cardigan's illness, she is allowed absolutely no visitors."

"It's the nature of the illness that I'm curious about."

"We can make no statement about that at this time, sir."

"Dr. Habib already told me it was a virus," said Dan.

"Is it a viral illness?" Jake asked the android.

"We can make no statement about that at this time, sir."

"Okay, then can you switch me to someone who's authorized to make a statement?"

"Not at the present moment, sir."

"What about Dr. Habib—where can I find him?"

"Because of his caseload, Dr. Habib is unable to leave the Isolation Wing. Is there anything else I can do to be of assistance, sir?"

"Nope."

The smiling doctor faded, replaced by Kate. She was alone in her room now.

"I thought you could maybe find out something, Dad."

"I will, but I'm going to have to make a few calls first. Put a little pressure on the hospital crew."

"Phones are just over there." Dan pointed across the room. "She's not . . . you saw her . . . you don't think she's going to die?"

"No, don't worry. I don't think she's going to die," he told his son. But he lied.

:: 14 ::

The director of the Isolation Wing was not happy. A tall, thin man of fifty, he sat, impatiently, behind his white desk, frowning across at Jake and Beth. "I don't mind saying," he said, "that I dislike being manipulated."

"We realize that," said Beth, smiling faintly at him. "But since you refused to see Mr. Cardigan, even after several of his influential contacts suggested it, I decided I had to step in."

"Simply because you happen to have gone to school with the daughter of our chief of staff doesn't really—"

"Suppose I just ask my questions, Dr. Goedewaagen," put in Jake. "You can answer them and then we can break up this meeting."

Goedewaagen aimed a scowl at Jake. "Very well, but keep in mind that I am only doing this because I was ordered to by—"

"I want to know about my former wife."

"She's extremely ill."

"That I saw. Can you tell me what it is she's suffering from?"

The doctor paused to glare at Beth. Finally he said to Jake, "It had been decided, after discussing the entire situation with the local and state governments, to keep this whole situation quiet as long as possible. But since I'm being pressured . . . Your wife, Mr. Cardigan, has fallen victim to a very dangerous and highly contagious virus."

"What is it?"

Dr. Goedewaagen rubbed at the side of his nose. "We don't

know. It appears to be something no one has encountered previously, not even the Disease Monitoring Stations around the world."

Jake leaned forward in his chair. "Is it a synthetic virus, something cooked up in a lab?"

After a few seconds the doctor nodded. "It appears to be, yes. Though thus far we haven't been able to identify it."

"But Kate isn't the only one who has this, is she?"

Turning away from them, the doctor replied, "During the past week there have been over a hundred cases brought into this hospital alone. Every other medical facility in San Francisco has admitted similar numbers with these identical symptoms."

"What are the symptoms?"

"The victim is stricken with a sudden and extremely high fever. Dizziness and then disorientation follow, along with, in most cases, severe vomiting. Within a few hours the majority of them fall into a semicomatose state and remain that way. The respiratory system is also affected and normal unaided breathing becomes impossible."

Beth asked, "Have there been cases elsewhere—in other states or in other parts of the world?"

"Except for a few spillover cases across the bay in Marin County and down on the Peninsula, no."

Jake said, "That means that the virus, whatever it is, has only been turned loose in Frisco."

"That's our present suspicion."

"Any idea who's behind it—or why?"

"We assume it's the work of a terrorist group." Dr. Goedewaagen shook his head. "As yet, however, no one has claimed responsibility or made any demands."

Beth nodded at Jake. "Dr. Chesterton," she said quietly.

"What's that?" asked the doctor.

"Nothing."

Jake asked him, "What about a cure?"

"So far nothing we've tried works," answered Dr. Goedewaagen. "As of yesterday there have been forty-seven deaths throughout the city and no patient has shown any sign of improvement. If we can

identify the virus—we suspect it may be something that was originally developed in a government lab somewhere—then we may be
able to determine the antidote. We, naturally, have queries out to
various government agencies, asking for help. Otherwise . . ."

"Can't you develop a cure on your own?"

"The whole idea of a synthetic virus, Miss Kittridge—the reason
they were developed to use as weapons—is that the enemy you use
them against won't be able to come up with a quick cure. These are
planned diseases, designed to outwit researchers. Given enough
time, weeks at least, we can, almost certainly, come up with something."

"But how long do the victims live?" asked Jake.

"It varies with the patient," answered the doctor. "We've had
some who managed to survive for only two or three days. In the case
of your wife, Mr. Cardigan—where the patient is relatively young
and healthy—we anticipate she will live for as long as ten days or
two weeks. Keep in mind, though, that we haven't had much experi-
ence with this and our calculations may be off." He shrugged, leaning back in his chair.

"You mentioned that this was highly contagious," said Jake.
"What about my son's catching it?"

"I'm glad you brought that up," Dr. Goedewaagen said. "We've
just decided—in fact I was called away from that staff meeting to
come here—we've decided that anyone who's had prolonged contact
with a plague victim ought to be kept here in our Observation Wing.
That way we can monitor them."

"You used the word plague," said Beth. "Is that what this is?"

"An epidemic, a plague, I'd say so. The number of victims has
kept increasing. In a few more days, perhaps sooner, we won't be
able to keep this a secret and panic will be added to the other
problems. The media are already starting to ask questions."

"You'd like my son to stay here then?"

"We can't legally require that, not at this stage of the situation.
But I think it would be best."

"Yeah, so do I. I'll talk to Dan." Jake stood up. "And maybe I
can find the antidote to this plague."

"What we need, Mr. Cardigan, is qualified medical experts, not impetuous private detectives."

Beth said, "I'd bet on Jake if I were you, doctor."

∎

The redhead reached across the narrow table, touching the control pad. The stripper vanished just as she was removing her final bit of clothing. "I can tell you how it ends," said the redhaired young woman as she sat, uninvited, across from Gomez.

Gomez said nothing.

The redhaired intruder continued, "If you know me, which you most certainly do, Gomez, you're aware I'm no stickler for ceremony. Still and all, however, I don't believe I'm straying out of line to any great degree, which every single person I deal with in the course of an average busy day might not agree with, when I suggest to you that a cordial greeting wouldn't be out of order under the present circumstances. Here we are, afterall, thrown together by fate, as it were, far from our native planet, hurtling through the vast void of—"

"Hi, Natalie, old chum," said Gomez, frowning at her. "Go away."

Smiling, Natalie Dent placed both sharp elbows on the tabletop and stared intently at him. "I've always harbored the suspicion, ever since I first encountered you back when you were a hardbitten SoCal state cop and I was a sweet and innocent, well, anyway sweet, young rube reporter working the police beat on the Greater Los Angeles *Fax-Times,* that you didn't exactly approve of me, which was okay by me, since my innate shyness does often get mistaken for aloofness and cause certain sorts of men, especially those who fancy themselves womanizers, don't approve—"

"*Vamos,*" suggested Gomez, making a go-away motion with one hand. "Depart, Nat. Take your leave, fold your tent, hit the road."

"Gee, a bilingual brushoff. That's very interesting, Gomez, because it indicates to me, and I think that I'm perfectly capable of being objective when the occasion arises to—"

"Natalie, really now, scram," he urged in a lowered voice. "A reporter for Newz, Inc., that godawful twenty-four-hour vidwall news service, ought not to be noticed blabbing away in public with a noted private investigator. Especially not while aboard a shuttle speeding toward a dive like The Casino."

"Oh, there's no need at all to worry about that, since I happen to have a perfect cover story for why I'm making this little jaunt," Natalie told him. "See, I'm supposed to be investigating a reliable rumor that Victoria Dorado, the madcap heiress who's run off once again, is up at The Casino throwing away another chunk of money from her seemingly bottomless coffers. So if anyone—for example, that husky bushy-browed thug slumped over at the bar and glowering at us with suspicion in his beady little eyes—does recognize me, why, I'm ready with a perfectly winning and convincing excuse for my actions and so no one will suspect, not even for a fleeting moment, that I'm heading there for exactly and precisely the same reason you are."

Gomez, resisting the impulse to turn and scan the bushy-browed thug, said, "Well now, *chiquita,* talk about coincidences. It so happens the Cosmos Agency has been retained to locate Miss Dorado and we, too, have had a tip that she's frequenting The Casino. Well, now that we both know what's afoot—*adiós.*"

The redhead sucked in one cheek and eyed him. "Isn't that something? Why, Gomez, you still think of me as the naive little hick from the Fresno Sector, and so easy to fool, as I was back at the age of nineteen when first we met. Well, listen, I'm twenty-six now and quite capable of spotting the truth behind a lot of—"

"Nat, are you capable of getting the hell away from me? You may well have turned into a deft, savvy reporter, but I don't want you hovering around me."

"I hope you don't think I'm displaying some sort of seedy sexual attraction toward you, Gomez, because as far as I'm concerned your type of curlyhaired egocentric wiseoff who falsely thinks he's fatally attractive to any and all women is precisely the sort of man I want nothing to do with, at least in any romantic kind of way. So don't flatter yourself."

"Great, I'll abandon all my foolish notions about your yearning for me." Gomez popped to his feet. "Farewell now, Natalie and, *por favor,* don't tag along with me for the remainder of this flight or after we hit The Casino. You have my solemn word that soon as I spot the Dorado lass, I'll give you a holler."

Standing, Natalie came around to take hold of his arm. "We can go to my cabin and talk things over. I've already debugged the place."

"We have nothing, absolutely *nada,* to chat about, dear lady."

"Sure, we do, so quit being obtuse," she advised. "For all you know, I already have a lot more information than you do on this upcoming Teklord meeting."

Gomez reflected on that. "Okay, we'll go talk."

"I told you we would."

15

Fog was rolling in across the dark bay. Dan stood near the see-through wall, hands deep in his trouser pockets and shoulders hunched, watching the mist swallow up the lights of the floating restaurants and the wateredge buildings. "What do you mean—that you can't do anything to help her?" he asked his father without looking at him.

"No, that's not it. I'm pretty sure I know what's behind the plague," Jake told him.

"I'm sorry, Dad, but it just sounds to me like you don't really have much of an idea about why she's dying."

"I'm going to find out who's behind this."

"But how long is that going to take you? A week—a month? Mom's going to be dead in a few days unless somebody can do something." Dan turned to face him. "I've been talking to some of the other visitors and nobody who has this lasts very long." He gestured toward the monitor screens. "One kid, about my age . . . Jesus, his father died while he was watching him on one of these damn screens. His father died and the screen just went blank. I don't want that to happen to—"

"It won't." He reached out to take his son's hand.

The boy jerked back from him. "Hey, watch it. You don't want to touch me. You might get contaminated and they'll lock you up here, too."

"Nobody's locking you up. But being here under observation is safer than—"

"And this way you won't have to take the responsibility of looking after me yourself."

"Look now, Dan, I love you and I'm concerned about you. But nobody, not even the doctors, knows what this virus is yet. By staying right here, you'll be—"

"That's okay, Dad, I've got no place else to go anyway. And this is better than school."

"Anytime you want to contact me, just call the agency number in GLA. They'll know where I am."

"I don't know if I'll need to contact you unless . . . unless Mom gets worse."

"Whenever you want to talk to me, for whatever reason, start with the Cosmos Detective Agency," Jake said, taking a step back from him. "This isn't the place to do it, Dan—but sometime, soon probably, we're going to talk about what really happened down across the border in Mexico."

"I know all about that, about Bennett's getting hurt and—"

"There are, though, a lot of things you don't know."

Dan looked again out into the foggy night. "Maybe your side of the story is different, maybe it's true," he said. "But I can't handle hearing it right now, Dad."

"Okay, sorry." Jake patted him on the shoulder. "I'll come see you again soon as I can."

"If you want to . . ." His son went walking away from him.

■

The hotel was built out over the water on the Berkeley side of the bay. Their rooms were high up in one of the towers.

"There's nothing to see out there but fog," mentioned Beth.

"I didn't notice." Jake came away from the living room window. He sat in a black armchair.

"The plague has to tie in with Gordon Chesterton some way," she said.

"What?"

"Chesterton's biological weapon must be responsible for the plague that's hit San Francisco."

Jake stood up again, went to the window and stared out. "I've got to tell you something."

"That's allowed."

"It's . . . well, when I saw Kate lying there with all those medical gadgets hooked up to her, looking so close to death . . . Beth, I really didn't feel anything." Crossing over to the black chair, he sat again. "There was the woman I'd been married to for fifteen years, she was dying. Sure, I felt some pity, a little sadness. That was about all."

"What did you expect to feel?"

"I'm not sure, just more than I did. I loved her, very much, once."

"Once isn't now."

"I just feel that—because of Dan—I ought to have showed more . . ." He shrugged, sighing.

"Why would you want to put on an act for your son?"

"To impress him. To make him like me again."

Beth said, "Dan doesn't know what you know, Jake, and maybe he never will. Your wife's lover, Bennett Sands, helped frame you and get you sent up to the Freezer for what was supposed to have been a fifteen-year sentence."

"Yeah, and I'm near certain Kate helped him set me up for that."

"So it doesn't really seem unnatural to me that you wouldn't exactly love her any longer."

"I don't want Dan to find out about any of that, but I can't exactly pretend I feel about Kate the way I did before the Freezer."

"But that's still the father he remembers," she said. "Working all this out, though, and getting to know you again is going to be as much Dan's job as yours."

"I'm anxious to help that happen, to speed it along."

"You probably can't."

"The way he looked at me over at the hospital, Beth, when I told him he'd have to stay there. It was pretty rough."

"I'm probably not the best person to be giving you advice on this," she said. "Since I don't especially get along with my own father these days."

"In your case you're pretty much convinced he was in cahoots with Sands and Hokori."

"I believe he was, yes," she said. "What you have to keep in mind about Dan is that he feels betrayed by you. Same way I feel about my father."

"But I never betrayed him or—"

"What he *feels* and what you *did* don't have to match exactly. From what you've told me, he was very hurt when you were arrested, tried and sentenced to the Freezer. To him, up to then, you'd been perfect—a hero policeman, a loving father. Then it turned out you were supposed to be a crook, a Tek dealer and worse. That must've been devastating, especially to a boy of ten or eleven."

"I was framed. I've been cleared and Dan knows it."

"Jake, logic and what the revised record shows now don't have much to do with this," she pointed out. "It's what Dan went through back then that's important. Eventually, hopefully, he'll see that you weren't to blame. Going to take time."

"We may not have time. It's possible Dan has the virus, too."

"You don't know that, nobody does."

Jake took a deep breath. "Okay, the best thing I can do is get to work on finding who's behind the plague."

"It has to have something to do with Dr. Chesterton, with the zombie killings and all. I don't believe this is a coincidence."

"If someone got hold of Chesterton's synthetic virus and decided to use it, they'd want to silence anybody who knew how to come up with a cure."

"That would include Dr. Mildred Rhodie and Colonel Keazby."

"And probably Winterguild, since he was starting to follow up rumors about this, apparently."

"But why try to kill you?"

"They may have done that for some entirely different reason."

"Or they might have figured, when you started looking for Winterguild's informants, that you were on the same trail."

"What we have is the Teklords turning loose a manmade virus on San Francisco. They wanted to make sure anyone who could stop the spread of the plague was out of the way," said Jake. "Why are they doing it?"

"Terrorism doesn't need a motive, does it?"

"It does, sure. It may turn out to be a crazy reason, but there's always a motive." Jake stood, began pacing the large oval living room of their suite. "The Teklords want something. They figure if they kill enough people and then promise to stop that they'll get what they want."

"But what do they want? It can't be my father's anti-Tek system, because they must know that's a long way from being ready to go."

"I wouldn't rule that out, but my notion is that, yeah, they have a more immediate objective."

"Then why haven't they made it known?"

"They're not ready. Not enough people have died."

"What's the next step for us?"

"I'll contact Bascom, since I'm sure this is linked with the Winterguild case, and tell him I'm going to stay here a day or so," Jake said. "Then I'm going to look up some of my contacts and informants in Frisco."

"San Francisco is going to be a very dangerous city from now on."

Jake grinned. "Greater Los Angeles hasn't been all that safe for me lately either," he said.

:: 16 ::

J ake was, he realized, alone in bed. According to the floating ball-clock up near the ceiling, it was a few minutes past seven in the morning. Yawning once, scratching at his ribs, he sat up. "Beth?" he called as he swung off the hovering airfloat bed.

"In here."

He followed her voice into the living room of their hotel suite. "Something?" he asked.

She was, fully dressed now, sitting in the vidphone alcove. "I thought of someone who might have some pertinent information, and it turns out he does." Smiling, she left the phone. "Friend of mine who teaches at UC here in Berkeley, in the Neobio Department."

"A guy?"

"Yes, and handsome, too. But that isn't why I left your side at such an early hour to contact him." She came over, put her arms around him and rested her head against his bare chest. "He used to know Gordon Chesterton down in GLA, and he suggested we look up a neobiologist named Jordon Belarski."

"Jordon and Gordon," muttered Jake. "Where do we find him?"

"Well, that's the problem. Belarski was teaching at UC until about two years ago, when he had some kind of breakdown. My friend called it a crisis of conscience, but he likes to use phrases like that." Beth moved back from Jake. "Belarski, when last heard from, was living a nomadic street life over in Frisco."

"I'll see if I can run the guy down. Would his crisis have anything to do with the biological weapons Chesterton was developing?"

"My friend says Belarski worked closely with Chesterton, although I don't recall ever having heard of the man before," she said. "I'm going up to UC later to have lunch with him and see what else I can find out. If that's okay with you?"

"Sure, I don't want you coming along to Frisco because—"

"I know, the city isn't safe for someone as fragile as I am."

"Exactly," he said, grinning.

■

At a vidphone booth in a transit station deep under the bay Jake, alone now, put through a call to the Marina Hospital. He reached the same smiling blond android doctor he'd spoken to the night before. "How's my former wife doing?" he asked after identifying himself.

"There has been no change in her condition, Mr. Cardigan."

"What about my son?"

"He's still in Observation and no symptoms of infection have developed. We would, however, suggest that he remain here for at least another two days."

Jake let out his breath. "Yeah, that's fine," he said. "Can I talk to him?"

"Hold on, please. I'll transfer you."

The screen went blank.

There were few people in the grey and black underground station. Not more than ten or so waiting for the next tubetrain to San Francisco.

The screen remained blank.

A fat man in the next booth was arguing loudly. "I tell you, Frances, I don't think it's safe for me to hop over there to Frisco. The stories I've been hearing . . . Listen, just because they're friends of mine and not friends of yours doesn't mean they don't know what's what. . . . It's bubonic plague or worse. . . . Of course I'm fond of your goddamn mother, but we can buy the old biddy a present someplace where I won't run the risk of . . ."

"Dad, have you found out anything?" Dan, looking pale and weary, was on the screen.

"I think I'm getting closer, but I still don't have the answer. How are—"

"But you really think there's some kind of cure for what Mom has?"

Jake nodded. "Sure, and we're getting closer to finding it," he said. "Keep in mind, too, that a lot of other people are working on this."

Glancing off to his left, Dan lowered his voice. "Do you believe that Mom is really still alive?"

"Of course she is. Why would you suspect—"

"I don't know, they give you so much bullshit around here," his son said. "And they mostly treat me like I was still a little kid. What did they tell you about Mom?"

"That there's no change in her condition."

"No change," echoed Dan sadly. "Yeah, that's what they keep telling me."

"It means she's not getting any worse, Dan."

"But no better, either." He shook his head. "I don't know what to believe."

Jake said, "I have to catch a train. I'll call you soon again."

"Can you help Mom, do you think?"

"Her and everybody else who's got this."

"It's too bad that I'm not really a kid anymore. Back then I still used to believe you'd keep all the promises you made to me."

"I'll keep this one."

"I hope so." He ended the call.

A minute and a half later the five-car train came gliding silently to a stop at the grey platform.

Jake stepped into the nearest car, which held only three other passengers. One of them was a priest dressed in black.

Jake sat down just as the train started up again.

"We'll be all right, Raymond," a thin woman across from him was saying. "We'll call Dr. Reisberson just as soon as we're back home at the condo."

The man beside her was slumped, his face darkly flushed, speckled with perspiration. "No . . . there's not going to be . . . enough time." His head fell forward, hitting against the back of the next seat. He began retching, his body shaking violently.

"My god." The woman pressed her hand against his back, trying to comfort him.

"Ma'am," said the plump priest, leaving his seat to walk over to her. "You'd best move away from him."

"He's my husband, he's terribly sick."

"What he's suffering from is very dangerous. You can catch it, too."

"I'm not afraid of that."

"Trust me, ma'am. Just step aside now and I'll summon the train's medibot."

"If I can only get him home, he'll be fine. We'll call our own doctor to look after him. Dr. Reisberson lives right in the same tower as—"

Her husband stopped vomiting, stopped shivering. He made a sad, keening noise before falling to the floor of the rail car.

His wife started to kneel down next to him, but the plump priest caught her by the arm and pulled her into the aisle. "It really is best if you touch him as little as possible."

"I've got to help him." She pulled free, dropped to her knees beside the fallen man. "Raymond, we're more than halfway home now. You can hold on until we get there. I'll help you sit back up in the seat and—"

"Ma'am, he's dead," the priest told her.

"No, he's not. Stop talking like that."

Jake suggested, "Why not go fetch the medibot and leave her alone?"

"My profession calls for aiding the troubled."

"She can't use any aid from you right now."

"Perhaps you're right." The priest turned, walked along the aisle to the middle of the car and touched a white wall plate with a red cross glowing on it.

A shrill wailing sound started.

"He's not dead," insisted the kneeling woman.

■

At a few minutes before noon Jake was walking down through Chinatown Park. The day was clear and bright, a mild wind rattled the leaves of the imitation trees.

"Good to see you again after so long, Jake." A slim, dapper Chinese of about forty was sitting on an orange bench, smiling at the approaching Jake.

"You're looking very . . . what's the word I need, Vince?"

"Elegant?"

"You're looking elegant. Though maybe that isn't the right word for describing a San Francisco cop."

Vincent Mok left the bench, brushing at his trousers. "You mentioned on the phone that you had some questions for me."

"I appreciate your taking the time," Jake said as they started walking along a curving path in the small block-square park. "I'm interested in a guy named Jordon Belarski. He used to be a fairly successful neobiologist over at UC, but he had a breakdown. Supposedly he ended up on the streets here in Frisco. Since you're in charge of the Street Life Division of the SF Police, Vince, I'm hoping you can—"

"Belarski, sure." Mok nodded. "Yeah, I know the professor. He likes to lecture people about the meaning of life and what morality is. Not surprisingly, most people don't want to hear about any of that and Belarski gets beaten up every now and then." He slowed, grew thoughtful, studied Jake. "What sort of case are you working on for Cosmos?"

"Started as a simple investigation into the causes of Kurt Winterguild's death, but—"

"He was a putz."

"True," agreed Jake. "The point is, Vince, this is starting to look as though it's tied in with your plague."

"I just heard your wife has it. I'm sorry about—"

"Exwife."

"Really? I didn't know. When did that happen?"

"While I was away. Any idea where I can find the professor?"

A skyambulance went roaring by low overhead, siren howling.

"Must be another plague victim." Mok pointed at the flying ambulance with his thumb.

"Any idea what's behind the plague?"

"It's manmade. But what the motive for turning it loose on us is, I don't know. And so far, nobody's popped up to take credit," said the policeman. "Before Belarski went totally bonkers and became a sidewalk philosopher—he was working on biological weapons, wasn't he?"

"Yep, as an associate of Dr. Gordon Chesterton."

"Ah, the noted wifekiller. Well, at least we don't have to worry about Chesterton, since he's safely on ice up in the Freezer and won't be out again until we're all old and grey." Mok paused. "The professor wanders around a lot, but in the past few weeks he's been living over in the Ruins."

"The Ruins?"

"Happened while you weren't around, I guess. An aftereffect of the Big Quake of 2117. Most of the Tenderloin area just toppled over," explained Mok. "What with one thing and another, having to do with budget and insurance problems, the city fathers and mothers haven't gotten around to rebuilding. It's possible nobody will get around to it for years to come. Meantime large quantities of homeless drifters, smalltime crooks, louts and loons have taken to squatting there."

"Do you police them?"

"A little, though mostly we simply try to make sure they don't come charging out of there to annoy our decent citizens. At last count, by the way, we had something around twenty-six decent citizens left in our fair city. You figure Belarski is tangled up with this plague in some way?"

"I sure want to talk to him about that possibility."

"Let me know what the guy has to say—providing any of it comes out coherent."

"Come along with me if you want. I could use a guide."

"No, when the denizens of the Ruins spot me, it usually inspires them to fling brickbats and assorted other samples of architecture. Despite my elegant appearance and winning ways, I'm not especially popular over there."

"Hard to believe."

Mok asked, "You have a kid, don't you?"

"One, yes."

"Boy or girl?"

"Boy, fifteen."

"Where is he?"

"Right now he's at the Marina Hospital, too. In Observation. There's a possibility he may develop what Kate's got."

"That's not good," he said, shaking his head. "How do you two get along?"

After a few seconds Jake answered, "Just great."

⁝⁝ 17 ⁝⁝

The Ruins stretched across ten square blocks. Jake entered the tumbledown area just as the day was starting to fade, making his way along what had once been Mason Street. There was now only a narrow twisty path zigzagging through enormous mounds of rubble. Piles that mingled bricks, shattered timbers, twists of metal rods, jagged fragments of plastiglass rose up all around. Here and there portions of walls still stood, with a few windows and doors still in place.

The twilight brought a chill wind with it, wisps and tatters of fog were beginning to drift across the Ruins. Jake saw a scatter of lights, portable electrolamps mostly, and a few cookfires.

In the gaping doorway of what was left of a liquor shop two thin women in ragged dresses were struggling with each other, punching and cursing. Sprawled at their feet was a deadman in a tattered raincoat.

"I saw him first," insisted one of the women as she jabbed the other, hard, in the ribs.

"Bullshit, honey. I did."

"He's mine. Whatever he's got on him is mine."

"Oh, you don't really want him, dear. Look, he's puked all over himself. I bet he's got the plague."

"Plague or drunk, I want what's in his pockets."

Jake continued on his way.

Near a great tumble of debris that had a lightsign reading ELM

HOTEL protruding from it midway up, three lean boys of about eleven or twelve were cleaning a bird that was probably a seagull. A small cookfire sputtered nearby.

Halting, Jake said, "I'm looking for Belarski."

"Go sod yourself," suggested the smallest and dirtiest of the trio.

"Five bucks," said Jake.

"Sod yourself twice," said another.

The third boy straightened up, wiping his bloody knife on the leg of his tattered grey trousers. "Make it ten."

"If you take me to him."

"Horseshit. I ain't going off alone with you, buddy. You look to me like the sort who comes into the Ruins so he can bugger sweet young tykes such as me."

"Just tell me where to find Belarski then," said Jake.

"You mean the professor, don't you?" inquired the smallest and dirtiest. He was still holding the gutted bird by its neck.

"That's the one."

"Always spouting a lot of crap about the dignity of man and the meaning of life."

Jake nodded. "Where is he?"

"Not far off." Dropping the bloody bird to the ground, he held out a dirty hand. "Pay me."

"For ten dollars," said Jake, "I need a little more in the way of directions."

The boy said, "You go straight along this passway for about a half mile, see. You'll come to a piece of a building that's got a sign out front saying PETE'S BARBER SHOP & WHOREHOUSE. Right around the corner from that there's what's left of a public fountain and a bit of grassy park. The professor's usually there this time of night, preaching away."

Jake passed him a Banx note. Then, as the two other boys closed in on the smallest, said, "I'll be coming back this way, fellows. He'd better still have his money."

The boy with the knife smiled thinly. "Oh, sure. We won't pick on Danny."

"That your name?" asked Jake.

"Maybe."

"Not a bad-sounding name."

"Mine's Wally," volunteered the one with the knife.

"Not bad either." Jake resumed walking. "Don't hurt him, Wally."

"Sure. Oh, sure. You got my word."

Laughter followed Jake.

The fog was rolling in thicker, pouring down over the dark piles of rubble and the jagged fragments of walls, filling up the narrow passway. Off somewhere, unseen, a cat suddenly cried out in pain.

"Stick him again, he ain't dead. Shit, he scratched me!"

"Hold him still, hold the bugger still or we'll miss dinner."

Off to Jake's right something went scurrying through a tumbled building.

After a few minutes he heard a voice.

". . . are we put on this Earth? You've asked yourselves that often. I know I have. Well, I've thought a lot about the answer. I've thought a lot about the answer. The purpose of life is to be kind to one another. To help each other . . ."

Jake saw him now.

It was, judging by the few photos he'd been able to dig up, Jordon Belarski, formerly of the University of California at Berkeley and prior to that an associate of Dr. Gordon Chesterton. The man was tall, gaunt, with curly blond hair that stood up high. He was wearing faded pants, at least five ragged sweaters, one on top of the other, and around his long, thin neck was wound a new-looking scarf of bright crimson.

Belarski was mounted up on a low pile of bricks near a patch of dry grass. He was shaking his fist as he spoke, staring intently into the mist as though there were an audience surrounding him. But there was no one at all attending his lecture.

". . . yes, I know what it is to betray your purpose, to spoil your life by compromising what it is that you—"

"Professor Belarski?" Jake had stopped a few feet from him.

"Save your questions until after my talk."

"I want to ask you about Gordon Chesterton."

Belarski executed a quick ducking motion. He started blinking rapidly, shaking his head, slowly, from side to side. "As I was saying," he went on, looking away from Jake and concentrating on another section of his invisible audience, "the essential truth, the only truth of life, is betrayal. First we betray—"

"This is important." Jake moved up close to him. "You may be the only one left who can help—a lot of people are going to die otherwise."

A look of pain touched Belarski's face and he made a brushing motion at the swirling mist. "They're already dead. Yes, it's much too late to stop that now. Oh, by preaching to the crowds, I can sometimes—"

"We've got to talk about Chesterton."

"Chesterton?" He shivered, his whole body rattling. Then he reached up and unwound the crimson scarf. "Perhaps you're the one," he said in a quieter voice.

"The one you can confide in?"

"Yes, I've concluded that I ought to explain to someone about the awful things I've done."

"Along with Chesterton?"

Belarski wrapped the scarf around his left hand. "They told me it was my duty, but they were wrong. Gordon tried to . . . Did you say you knew Gordon?"

"Only by reputation."

"An evil man. . . . I found that out much too late. But extremely convincing. Gordon swore to me that XP-203 was essentially a good thing." He stopped talking, turned his head away and stared into the fog. "I seem to have forgotten so much. Maybe that's what life is about . . . forgetting."

"Please," said Jake, "try to remember about XP-203."

"They told me it was the sort of biological weapon that would, of course, never actually be put to use. Yes, one that would only serve to frighten and intimidate the enemy—whoever the enemy might be at the moment." He sighed. "They used it in Brazil, did you know that?"

"No."

"We killed 3,648 people, children among them. 964 children under the age of ten. XP-203 got out of hand, they explained. It was only supposed to kill a few troops, as a demonstration of its potential. Got out of hand. 964 kids."

Jake asked him, "Is XP-203 Chesterton's synthetic virus?"

"Chesterton's and mine."

"You perfected the stuff—it worked?"

"964 kids. Yes, it worked."

"But XP-203 was supposed to have been destroyed years ago, wasn't it?"

"So they told us."

"Could any of it have survived? Could someone have access to a supply or manufacture new—"

"Have you ever wondered what we are placed on Earth for? Do you think it could be so that we can kill 964 children, none over the age of ten?"

Jake took hold of Belarski's arm. "Did you and Chesterton also develop an antidote?"

"There's no antidote for the awful things I've done."

"An antidote for XP-203?"

"The United States government never accepts a new lethal virus unless you provide a . . . But that's of no importance now. My mission now is to preach to the multitudes."

Tightening his grip, Jake said, "I'm near certain your XP-203 is what's being used here in Frisco. You know how to stop it."

"Do I?" He pressed the wadded-up crimson scarf to his chest. "I wasn't aware that the government had any further use for my services. How many children do they want killed this time?"

"You'll have to come with me, to explain to—"

"You don't understand. My mission now is to preach."

Belarski died then.

The beam of a lazgun came darting out of the thick surrounding fog. It touched his chest just above where he held the scarf and swiftly sliced through his torso.

Jake dived, hit the ground and rolled.

The beam came looking for him.

⁙18⁙

Jake got to his feet, went running into the fog. The beam of the lazgun hissed again, slashed across a pile of rubble three feet to his left.

He tripped on something unseen, fell, his head cracking into a fragment of wall. Jake scrambled around the wall, getting it between whoever it was out there in the misty night and himself.

This had been a small church, back before the Big Quake. There were still five rows of pews lined up on flooring that was strewn with chunks of mortar and thick with dust. The sole surviving stained glass window showed a handsome whiterobed angel with his wings unfurled.

The angel suddenly separated at the waist, his torso exploding into jagged chunks of glass and slamming down to the dusty floor.

The lazgun beam that had sliced the window in half came probing in at the new opening.

Jake, ducked low, ran along a row of seats and out through a great jagged gap in what was left of the opposite wall.

Beyond the collapsed church rose a high mound of debris that had once been a building. Beyond that there seemed to be nothing but chill, deadwhite fog.

Jake made his way around the pile, crouched behind it and drew out his stungun. He still hadn't seen who'd killed Belarski and was now stalking him. He didn't know how many of them were out there in the thick mist.

All at once a fat grey rat, frightened by something, ran out of the fog, brushed Jake's ankle and was gone.

Jake narrowed his eyes, watching the swirling mist. He spotted a dark blur that was moving, very slowly, closer. He aimed his stungun and fired. The humming beam of his weapon hit the shadowy shape.

There was a cry of pain, a shuffling sound of feet scraping on dirt. Someone fell against a pile of bricks, wooden beams and plastiglass.

Jake waited where he was, watching and listening.

A minute went by.

Jake stayed there for another full minute.

Then he started moving, circling the great mound of rubble. He listened as he went, straining to hear the faintest sound of pursuit.

Another partial building loomed up out of the fog. The entire front wall of Shery's Cafe stood, its front door hanging lopsided and half open.

When Jake was level with the door, it snapped all the way open, hitting his gunhand and sending the stungun spinning away into the fog.

A wide, black man lurched out. ". . . kill the bastard . . . Jake Cardigan . . ." He held a needlegun clutched in his left fist. "No good bastard has to die . . ."

Jake backed slowly, hoping he'd trip over his lost gun in time to use it on the zombie.

A knife sailed by Jake's head and hit the big man in the chest. The zombie gasped. His needlegun went off, sending two dozen sharp silver darts into the ground. With his right hand he made a grab for the hilt of the knife that was sticking in him. He missed, staggered. He made a second grab and missed again. His hand dropped to his side and, spitting out blood, he fell flat out on the ground and died.

"That's worth twenty," said a young voice. "At least."

Jake turned.

Wally, one of the boys he'd met by the cookfire, was walking out of the night mist. "I've been following you," he said as he stooped to retrieve his knife from the deadman's chest.

"Thanks."

"Pretty good toss of the knife, wasn't it?"

"Expert." Jake saw his stungun lying nearby and picked it up.

"You want an escort out of the Ruins?" Wally wiped the knife blade on the side of his trousers.

"Quiet a minute." Jake was looking back the way he'd come.

"There were only two of them."

"Sure?"

"The one you decked, he had the lazgun. This poor sod he brought with him," said Wally, kicking the deadman in the side with his battered shoe. "That's the lot."

Jake kept his stungun in his hand. "Here," he said, fishing out ten dollars in Banx notes with his other hand.

"For an additional twenty-five I'll see you all the way home," offered the boy.

"I can handle it alone."

Wally stared at him a minute, then shrugged and walked away.

■

The cyborg chef whispered, "Quick, along this way."

Natalie, clutching a small vidcamera to her chest, crouched and entered the metal-walled tunnel first.

Gomez, stepping around a large drum of soyflour and ducking, followed the redhaired reporter out of the galley pantry.

The chef, a fat blond man with a silver right arm, came last. "Tiptoe, please. Make no noise," he urged in a nervous whisper.

The tunnel, which was less than five feet high, slanted downward. There was no light except what drifted in from the partly open pantry panel behind them.

After they'd covered roughly a thousand feet the tunnel ended at a thick metal door.

"Excuse me, coming through," whispered the uneasy chef. He oofed around Gomez, squeezed by Natalie to the door. "I've a key someplace." With the forefinger of his flesh hand he pressed one of the buttons that ringed his metal wrist like a bracelet. "Darn, that's not it." An eggbeater had replaced the silvery metal fingers. "Hold on, patience. There." A large brassy key replaced the eggbeater.

The heavy door whirred slightly as it swung open inward.

"That made too much noise," whispered the anguished chef.

Beyond the doorway was a warm, musty room full of darkness. The chef slipped inside first, followed by Natalie and Gomez.

The detective said, "Can we turn on some lights now?"

"Not so loud. We could get killed if any—"

"Spike," cut in Natalie, "I appreciate your letting me bribe you to let us in here. But, if you don't mind my saying so, you're really making much too much over what is essentially a simple eavesdropping excursion."

"When I shut the door, Gomez," said Spike, "touch that light panel on your left."

"*Sí.*"

The door was shut, Gomez touched the panel and, after three or four seconds of blackness, light blossomed overhead. The small room had a bank of ten small vidscreens in the far wall with three chairs facing them.

"Some years ago, when the management was even less scrupulous, this place was used to monitor the activities in the more expensive suites aboard The Casino," explained the jittery cyborg, gesturing with his silvery metal fingers at the screens. "The meeting you're interested in watching is taking place in the Imperial Suite."

Natalie was already at the wall, studying the screens. "That'll be Screen 7." She reached out, touched a button.

". . . TERRIBLE FRIGGING BOOZE CONSIDERING WHAT WE'RE PAYING FOR THIS—"

"Turn it down!" The chef leaped, slapping at the control panel. "If anyone hears us we're finished."

"Has it ever been pointed out to you, Spike," inquired Gomez, "that your manner doesn't inspire confidence?"

"Come take a look," said Natalie, who was watching Screen 7. "The guy who's complaining is Sig Schraube."

"Yeah, the head man of the biggest Tek cartel in United Germany."

"You've got exactly one hour by the clock," whispered Spike. "I'll be back for you then." He let himself, quietly, out of the monitoring room.

The screen provided a long shot of a large living room. There were two black sofas and a half dozen plastiglass armchairs. At the moment there were six men in the room.

Natalie aimed her camera at the screen. "The man under the animated painting of the ballerina is Leopold Boreg, who controls Tek distribution in Israel."

"Also in attendance are Klaus Ruuvi of Finland and Manuel Parafuso of New Brazil."

"Both important Teklords."

"Let's listen." He upped the volume a bit.

". . . screw her," Ruuvi was saying. "There's no reason for her to think she can run our whole damn setup."

Boreg said, "She did, afterall, come up with the basic scheme, Klaus. And Tora also arranged for us to acquire a sufficient supply of XP-203."

"Tora?" Gomez frowned.

"Know the name?"

"Yeah, but it's supposed to be inscribed on a tombstone over in Japan."

". . . the purpose of this meeting," said Parafuso, "is to select the next target city, isn't it?"

"How about Rio?" suggested Boreg.

"That's not especially funny, Leopold."

"We don't have to pick another city yet—they may give in after Frisco."

Schraube was scowling at the glass in his big hand. "What's the latest report from San Francisco?"

"3,400 cases as of this morning," answered Ruuvi.

The German shook his head. "Far from enough."

"We've only just started. Keep in mind that the way this stuff works, the number of cases will keep multiplying. By this time next week there should be 15,000, the next week that'll jump to 45,000. At which point we make our first statement."

Boreg said, "That's waiting too long."

"It has to be that way, Leopold," insisted Ruuvi. "With only 3,000 some cases we haven't got them sufficiently scared. In two weeks there'll be not only 45,000 but, according to the figures I've been provided, 20,000 deaths as well."

"I agree," said Parafuso. "Two weeks from now, they'll be ready to concede. Then they'll agree to halt all interference with our distributing Tek and—"

"It's going to take more than 20,000 dead San Franciscans," said Schraube, "to get the United States to lay off, and to get them to persuade the rest of the world to go along."

"That's why we need a second target city," said Boreg. "A city in Europe somewhere."

"How about London?" said Parafuso. "A very smug city, and much too cold. If we use XP-203 there and produce, say, an additional 15,000 or so deaths—that ought to convince everyone."

Schraube sipped his drink, made a pained face. "The more time that passes, the more likely it is that they'll come up with an anti-dote."

"They won't, they can't," said Ruuvi. "XP-203 was specifically designed to outwit any and all—"

"I believe it can be done," said the German. "Especially if organizations like the Worldwide Health Agency become involved. You may recall that when this scheme of Tora's was first suggested, I told you all that I doubted we would have unlimited time."

"You persist in missing the essential fact about the virus," Ruuvi told him. "XP-203 can be modified as we go along. That's one of the beauties of it, Sig. Were they to find a cure for Strain 1, fine. We come back at them with Strain 2 and they have to start hunting for an antidote all over again. When they finally capitulate to us and make all the concessions we want, including the surrender of all notes and models on the Kittridge anti-Tek system, then we hand over the cure. But, should the bastards try to back down once they've got it, then we hit them with Strain 3 or Strain 4. We can't lose."

On his side of the wall, Gomez said, "I wonder if XP-203 is

something that Dr. Gordon Chesterton had a hand in a few years back."

"Hush, I want to hear this."

Across the room the door started to open. "Why's Spike coming back so soon?" asked Gomez, turning around.

The door opened fully. It wasn't Spike.

::19::

On the vidphone screen the same blond android medic was telling Jake just about what he'd told him the last time he'd checked with the Marina Hospital. "Mrs. Cardigan's condition remains virtually unchanged," he said from behind his neat white desk.

"She isn't any worse, though?"

"Nor is she any better. At this point there's no cause for either undue optimism or pessimism."

"And my son?"

"He continues in good health, with no symptoms."

"That's great. How long before you'll consider he's out of danger?"

"Another day or so. Is that all, Mr. Cardigan?"

"Yeah, thanks." The screen went blank, Jake leaned back in the alcove chair. Closing his eyes, he rubbed at his forehead with his fingertips.

The door to the hotel suite opened.

Jake jumped up, spun and reached into his jacket for his stungun. "Oh," he said, grinning and dropping his hand.

"Nice reflexes." Beth shut the door behind her. "Any news?"

"Kate's no better. Dan still isn't showing any signs of the plague."

"Did you talk to him?"

Jake shook his head. "I skipped that this time," he answered. "I don't want Dan to think I'm forcing myself on—"

"He doesn't think that," she said. "And he's coming around—eventually he's even going to forgive you."

"Forgive me? For what—being dumb enough to let Bennett Sands and Sonny Hokori frame me?"

Beth glanced up at a floating ball-clock. "I can allow you about two more minutes for selfpity, Jake," she said. "Then I really would like to tell you what I found out from my friend at UC."

Jake said, "Okay, I'll cut my sulking short. What?"

She sat on the sofa, crossed her legs. "His name is Ralph Jimgrin, by the way."

"That's pretty illuminating right there."

"Ralph knew both Chesterton and Belarski. He's been studying the San Francisco plague. He has friends at the National Disease Control Agency, so he was able to get reports from all the hospitals that are treating victims. Based on what Belarski told him, back when he was beginning to crack up, Ralph is fairly certain that the Chesterton synthetic virus is what's being used."

"XP-203." Jake started to pace. "What about supplies of the virus?"

"All supposedly destroyed years ago."

"Then how can somebody be using it in Frisco?"

"They're obviously able to manufacture it again."

"Does Jimgrin have any notion how they could do that? Was Chesterton's research preserved, stored somewhere?"

"All destroyed, too, as far as Ralph's been able to learn."

"Could Belarski have passed along the knowledge needed to whip up new supplies of the virus?"

"It's possible. But Ralph doesn't believe, considering what Belarski's moral stand had become, that he'd do anything like that."

"He could've been forced," said Jake. "What about the antidote?"

"I'm afraid that was destroyed, too, along with all of Chesterton's notes on it," said Beth. "Sounds like what we've hit is a dead end."

"No," said Jake. "Because Chesterton knows how to produce the antidote."

"But he's up in the Freezer and . . . Oh, yes, I see. He can be revived and questioned."

"I'm going to talk to Bascom. He'll finagle us a Reanimation Order and then we'll go to the Freezer."

"Are you up to doing that?" She watched his face. "That's not a place you—"

"Yeah, I can do it. I have to."

A pounding commenced on the door.

"Open up, Cardigan! I know you're in there! C'mon, c'mon!"

It was a woman's voice, but not one he recognized.

Another voice sounded in the hotel hallway. "Miss, step away from there, please." That was Agent MacQuarrie. "Now, very slowly bring your hands up and lock them behind your head."

"Dimwit, I'm an agent with the National Disease Control Agency."

"Even so, miss. Raise your hands while I frisk you."

"You're going to find yourself providing security for minor politicians during their tours of obscure Central American republics no later than this time tomorrow, dimbulb, if you so much as touch one finger to my person. Here, look over my ID packet and put that stupid stungun away."

Jake placed the voice finally. "Mixon," he said. "Onita Mixon."

"She's really with the NDCA?"

"Oh, yeah," he answered. "And there are two things in the world she hates—germs and me."

■

The man who stepped into The Casino monitoring room was just a shade over five feet tall. He was thin, swarthy and wore a tightfitting skyblue suit. His right hand was made of gunmetal.

Directly behind him came a lean black man carrying a lazrifle. Then two large, wide men in suits the same color as that of the small man entered. They were dragging Spike, the bribed chef.

Gomez said, "When they assigned me this cabin, they assured me I'd have undisturbed privacy while I—"

"Shut the fuck up," suggested the small man. He glanced from Gomez to Natalie. "You don't have much in the way of tits, sister."

"If you broke in here just to tell me that, I already knew." The redhead lowered her vidcam and edged nearer to Gomez.

The small man made a sniggering sound. "A couple of wiseasses," he observed, nodding at the tall black man. "We got us a couple of wiseasses, Leon. What do you think of our having a couple of wiseasses, Leon?"

"Not much, Buzzer."

Buzzer gave a rueful shake of his head. "Leon doesn't think much of you two wiseasses."

"I suppose we can trade badinage like this all the live long day," said Gomez. "But why don't you gents simply tell us—"

"Shut up!" Buzzer touched his wrist, then poked the curlyhaired detective in the side with his metal forefinger.

"Hey!" A fairly strong electric shock went knifing into Gomez's ribs, making him shake involuntarily.

Natalie said, "There's no need to—"

"You can shut up, too." Buzzer gestured at the two men who were holding the shivering Spike. "Bring the asshole over here."

"You don't understand," said the chef, whose lips were cracked and caked with blood. "I'm telling you, Buzzer, I never took any money from these—"

"Don't talk." Leon slapped him, hard, across the mouth.

Blood started running again, spilling down across his chin. "I'm trying to tell you guys that they forced me to—"

"Don't tell us." Leon hit him again.

Buzzer smiled at Gomez. "Which anti-Tek agency are you with?"

"I'm an operative with the Cosmos Detective Agency in Greater Los Angeles," Gomez told him. "The tip we had was that we could get a look into the suite of a lady who might be Victoria Dorado with this monitoring setup."

"Oh, and you picked up on the meeting by mistake, huh?"

"Must have, yeah. We were about to switch to—"

"These assholes think I got shit for brains, Leon."

"That's not so, Buzzer."

"Leon says I don't have shit for brains," said Buzzer. "And only somebody like that would believe your halfassed story."

"You're smart, I'm dumb," said Gomez. "We got a bad tip and walked into something."

"Not a good idea," said the black man.

"You hear that? Leon says it's not a good idea to kid with me," said Buzzer. "Pay attention now—I'm going to stash you away for about an hour. By then this meeting you've been eavesdropping on will be finished. Then a couple of the participants will want to talk with you. You'd be smart to forget about being wiseasses and get ready to tell the truth."

"I can tell you that right now."

Buzzer smiled, made a dismissive gesture with his flesh hand. "Let me give you a demonstration."

"Good idea," said Leon.

"Spike, tell these two assholes how good I am at getting answers."

"I told you all I know already. I never . . . Ow! Oh, Jesus!"

Buzzer had grabbed him suddenly in the crotch with his metal hand. The gunmetal fingers made crackling sounds as Spike screamed.

One of the men holding him laughed.

■

Buzzer decided to stay behind in the monitoring room with Spike, who was sprawled unconscious now on the floor. "I think I better ask him a few more questions. Is that a good idea, do you think, Leon?"

"Damn good, Buzzer. I'll stay, too." The long, black man pointed at Gomez and Natalie and then at the door. "Take them away, boys."

The pair of thugs escorted their prisoners back along the tunnel, through the pantry and the robot kitchen and into a long grey corridor.

At a metal door marked STOREROOM 6 they halted. One of the

heavyset men said, "Inside, assholes." He inserted an electrokey in the slot, the door hissed open.

Taking Natalie's arm, Gomez escorted her across the threshold. They were in a large metal-walled room with a fretted ceiling. Stacked neatly all around were about fifty deactivated female androids, still in costume. There were showgirls, waitresses, maids and even some lady wrestlers.

As the door shut on them, Gomez observed, "This, *chiquita*, offers possibilities."

::20::

he morning fog hung heavy around the Oakland Spaceport. Jake, fingers of his right hand drumming slowly on the arm of his plastiglass chair, was looking out through the window of the small waiting room next to the boarding ramp for the prisonbound shuttle.

Beth was sitting beside him. "You okay?"

"Tip-top."

"You've been looking somewhat downhearted."

"I almost always look that way," he told her, grinning. "You've just never noticed before."

"You told me once that the Freezer, the first time you saw it, reminded you of something. But you never got around to—"

"When I was a kid, actually about the same age Dan is now, I was sent to a school they called the Sky Academy."

"I've heard of that. A very strict military sort of place for . . . well, for boys with problems."

"I fit into that category. Or so my father thought."

"And your mother?"

Jake returned to watching the fog. "It didn't much matter what she thought. My father was a professional military man. He ran the show."

"I know."

"Guess I've told you most of this already." He fell silent.

Finally Beth asked, "How long were you up at that orbiting school?"

"Nearly two years. My mother got sick while I was at Sky Academy and . . . she died while I was up there." He shook his head. "Once I got clear of the place, I promised myself I'd never go near a setup like that again, that I'd never send my kids to one."

"So why is Dan at Oceanside?"

"Kate chose it," he said. "It doesn't actually orbit the planet, but it sure looks and smells like Sky Academy. Sending your son off to a school like that isn't—"

"Good morning, Cardigan." Onita Mixon, a slim black woman, had come striding into the Reception Room. Two large silverplated robots in white tunics trailed behind.

Jake rose. "Morning, Nita."

The National Disease Control Agency agent asked him, "You feeling any remorse yet?"

"Over what—the fact I've known you for almost ten years?"

"Ten minus the four you were up there." She pointed her forefinger at the ceiling. "No, Cardigan, I meant remorse over the fact you were willing to let thousands of people in Frisco die while you and the other crooks at Cosmos got hold of the cure first. That way you could peddle it to the—"

"Nita, you're going along to the Freezer," he reminded her. "There's no need to lecture me on the ethics of the Cosmos Agency or—"

"If it hadn't been for Jake," put in Beth, standing, angry, "nobody would yet know the probable cause of this damn plague. As soon as he talked to Chesterton, he was going to pass on whatever he found out."

Agent MacQuarrie had been standing across the room. Looking a little uneasy, he moved closer to the group.

Onita nodded to herself. "You're the one he's replacing his wife with, aren't you? It figures you aren't going to tumble to Cardigan's real motives."

"None of you people from NDCA, not one, even suspected that Chesterton's virus might be what was—"

"We did, though, and that's exactly what I've been digging into for almost two days—along with a lot of other possibilities," said the agent. "That's how I learned that Cosmos and that opportunistic Bascom had Jake hunting the antidote. I figure Cosmos would've sold it for as much as you could get."

"Onita, when you burst in on us last night, I agreed to cooperate," said Jake. "But our deal doesn't include my having to listen to your lectures."

"That's right, you must be uneasy about this trip this morning," she said, smiling. "From what I hear, you're damn lucky they didn't ship you straight back to the Freezer when you got home from Mexico."

Beth smiled, too. "Agent Mixon," she said, "Jake has a policy of not hitting women—but I don't. Go away now, please."

The agent studied Beth for a few seconds. "You do a pretty good job of covering for him." Shrugging, she walked over to where her robot associates were standing.

Agent MacQuarrie backed off, too.

Beth said, "I was about ready to slug her."

"I think she noticed."

From an overhead speaker a voice announced, "All prisoners have now been safely loaded aboard Shuttle Flight 21 for the penal colony. There is no danger to passengers and they may start boarding."

•

The desk recognized him. "Prisoner #19,587," said the half-circle gunmetal desk after the recog camera that was mounted on its top scanned Jake.

He was sitting in the steel visitor's chair in the center of the oval room. Everything here was grey. "I'm Jake Cardigan now," he corrected, spreading the various forms and permits he'd brought with him out on the desk. "I've got a Temporary Resurrect Order for Prisoner #18,977—Chesterton, Gordon. You've already been notified of that."

"Forgive me, yes. For just a moment there I thought you were coming back to stay with us again, Mr. Cardigan."

"You should have let me handle this." Onita Mixon was standing near the doorway of the Administration Office. "Your jailbird record is getting in the way of an efficient operation."

"Quit heckling," advised Beth, fists clenching at her sides.

Agent MacQuarrie tapped her on the shoulder, shaking his head. "We don't want an incident, Miss Kittridge."

The desk camera dipped on its coiled metal neck, scanning the forms Jake had spread out. "Everything appears in order," the vox-box said. "You'll be escorted to a Processing Room in the Resurrection Wing, Mr. Cardigan. You'll have to go alone, since we can't allow more than one person to be with the prisoner at a time."

"Hold on," said the NDCA agent. "He's sure not going to have first crack at this."

"After Chesterton's revived," Jake said, "he can be brought to an Interview Room. I won't ask him any questions until then."

"Who knows what he's liable to confide in you when he first wakes up?"

"When he first wakes up," Jake assured her, "he's not likely to be in any shape for confiding."

A grey panel in the grey wall slid silently open. A grey robot stepped two paces into the room. "I've come to escort Mr. Cardigan."

"Don't get too tricky," warned Onita as Jake stepped through the wall.

"I'll try not to."

■

Jake hesitated, for just a few seconds, on the threshold of the small Processing Room. Although it wasn't the same one, it was very similar to the chill, metal-walled room he'd awakened in just weeks ago, after his four-year stretch here in the Freezer.

"Something wrong, sir?" inquired his robot escort.

"Nothing, no." He went on in.

There was a white metal table at the room's center; dangling above it was an assortment of wires and tubes. There was a large gunmetal robot standing next to the table and, in the far corner, a single grey metal chair.

Jake felt some momentary tightness in his chest as he crossed the small, cold room.

His escort had remained in the corridor. "If you'll be seated, sir, the body of Prisoner #18,977 will be brought here immediately and the revival proceedings can begin."

"I'll stand and wait." He leaned against the chill wall.

The robot nodded and left.

A minute passed.

The big robot next to the white table didn't move.

Two more minutes went by.

The big robot turned its head toward the open doorway.

Another three minutes passed.

Jake walked over to the doorway, took a look along the corridor. There was no sign of anyone.

He went back and leaned against the wall.

A full nine minutes later a chromeplated robot in a grey suit came in. "Would you mind coming with me, Mr. Cardigan?"

"I'm supposed to be waiting here for Dr. Chesterton's arrival."

"We've experienced a slight snag."

"What sort of snag?"

"If you'll accompany me, an explanation will be provided."

"Okay." He moved to the door. "Nice meeting you," he said to the big robot beside the white table.

⠶ 21 ⠶

omez, pacing slowly, made a second circuit of the storeroom he and the redhaired reporter were imprisoned in. Shoulders slightly hunched, he stared in turn at the walls, the ceiling and the small grey disk he had resting in the palm of his hand. "Our dungeon isn't bugged," he announced as he dropped the disk into a coat pocket. "Good thing those louts didn't deprive me of this handy gadget."

"Now we can have, I suppose, a confidential conversation." Natalie was standing, arms folded, next to a stack of blonde showgirl androids. "Privacy is all well and good, but since we're on the brink of extinction, it's not, you won't mind my saying, the topmost concern on my—"

"Do you have a nailfile?"

"I do, yes, as a matter of fact. But again, Gomez, personal grooming isn't very important when you're—"

"May I, *por favor,* borrow the thing?" He made an impatient give-it-here motion with his left hand.

Natalie handed it over. "What are you intending?"

"You know Joe Waterloo?" Gomez quickly scanned the room, then went walking to where three hefty android lady wrestlers were stacked, face up, one atop the other. "Since we don't have much time, I'll start with the sturdiest available."

"I've found, in my few dealings with him, that Joe is a relatively reliable informant, but—"

"Joe's allowed me to watch him at work whilst he reactivated worn-out androids." Gomez hefted the topmost lady wrestler, a husky blonde in crimson tights, off the pile. He dumped her, as gently as possible, onto the storeroom floor. "The lessons that I learned at Joe's knee, coupled with my own natural mechanical knack, ought to enable me to revive a few of these ladies." He knelt and, using the borrowed nailfile, pried off a small flesh-colored plate in the andy grappler's back. "I've got to reanimate them, then modify a little to get them to follow our orders."

"Do you think you can accomplish that?"

"Before an hour has passed, *cara*, we'll know one way or the other."

■

Gomez sounded angry, his voice was raised. "Listen, *chiquita*, I've covered cases all over the world, on dozens of satellites and space colonies and even on the Moon. Until I hooked up with you I never had—"

"Keep in mind that I've won *prizes* for my clever outwitting of all sorts of scoundrels," cried Natalie, hands on hips.

They were standing near the door of their storeroom prison, facing each other and seeming to argue.

"I sure wouldn't hand you a prize."

"Don't you try to tell me I don't deserve my awards and honors."

The door hissed open, revealing the lean, black Leon and the two thugs who'd escorted them here an hour and five minutes ago.

"Oh, *sí*, you might get an award for being the most annoying bimbo in the universe!"

"You are, as I've long suspected, a dreadful person." The angry redhead swung out, slapping Gomez across the cheek.

Watching the quarrel, Leon didn't notice the big blonde android wrestler inching her way along the wall at the left of the doorway. He didn't become aware of her until she was hurtling through the air straight at him.

Her name, according to the engraving on the buckle of her wide golden belt, was Tessie the Torpedo.

Before the startled Leon could even touch his shoulder holster, Tessie had him down on the floor and was bouncing her broad backside on his narrow chest.

The two thugs allowed themselves to be diverted by this for roughly three seconds. Ample time for the two other lady wrestlers that Gomez had reactivated and modified to jump them.

The other blonde was known as Moonbase Minnie. The third andy, and the burliest of the lot, was called Killcrazy Maisie and had hair of glowing red.

Maisie dropkicked her selected hoodlum square in his chin. That caused him to grind his teeth, hop two feet into the air and flap his arms several times.

Maisie caught him before he touched down, lifted him up and executed a graceful airplane spin that ended with his flying into the far wall.

He slammed it with a rattling thunk. When he hit the floor, flat out, he was unconscious.

Tessie had by that time succeeded in breaking Leon's right arm and, by whapping his skull repeatedly against the metal floor, knocking him out cold.

Moonbase Minnie lifted the second thug in a crushing bear hug. He gasped, yelped, gasped again and passed out. She let go of him, stepped deftly aside as he toppled over.

Spitting on her hands and then rubbing them together, Minnie turned to Tessie. "I can hear you wheezing from here, dearie. You need an overhaul."

"I thought you were waltzing with your guy, sweetheart. He probably just passed out from fright after getting a gander at you."

"Listen, dearie, if I'd wanted to—"

"Ladies, *bastante,*" cautioned Gomez. "Keep in mind that I'm the leader of the group. Right now what we have to do is *vamos.*" Crouching beside the fallen Leon, he took his stungun, his lazgun and the labeled electrokey to one of The Casino's private shuttles.

Nodding toward the doorway, Natalie asked, "Can you ladies escort us to where they've got their ships docked?"

"A cinch, skinny," said Maisie. "Unless they've moved things around since they put us out to pasture."

"Pasture?" laughed Tessie. "The junkheap is where they tossed you, lovie."

"Ladies." Gomez opened the door to take a careful look out into the corridor. "We're operating on a very tight schedule today. It looks safe outside, so let's make our way to the dock *muy pronto.*"

Maisie gave Natalie a cordial nudge in the side. "How's this gink do in the sack, hon?"

"I don't have anything but hearsay information on that."

"He's sort of cute," observed Tessie.

"Except for that hair," said Minnie.

"To the docking area." Gomez stepped into the corridor and beckoned them to follow.

::22::

Two androids, three robots and a human were standing around something on the floor of the large grey room.

The human, a fat man with shortcropped blond hair and a bright pink face, stepped clear of the group to frown at Jake as he was escorted in. "What do you know about this, Cardigan?"

A darkhaired female andy and a chromeplated robot moved aside so that Jake could get a look at what they'd been circling. It turned out to be an opaque plastiglass coffin, the lid off and leaning against it. The coffin was empty.

Jake rubbed his thumb knuckle across his chin. "Is this where Chesterton was supposed to be reposing?"

"It is," said the fat man. "Would you have any idea where he is?"

Grinning, Jake replied, "Seems to me you folks are in a better position to answer that than I am."

"I'm Deputy Warden Silverman," the fat man said. "I was here while you were serving your sentence, Cardigan."

"We didn't meet at the time." He tapped the empty coffin with the toe of his boot. "I came up here to the Freezer—not a favorite spot of mine—specifically to talk to Chesterton. If I'd known in advance he was missing, I'd have spared myself the trip."

"He's not necessarily missing," said the deputy warden.

"It's possible," suggested the darkhaired female android, "that he's simply been misfiled."

"How often has that happened?"

"Never, but it remains a possibility."

Jake eyed the fat warden. "I've never heard of anybody escaping from up here."

"That would be impossible, since all our prisoners are kept in a state of suspended animation," said Silverman. "We also have a very efficient security system, no one could've broken in from outside and sprung him."

Jake nodded at the empty box. "How often do you check the coffins?"

"We prefer to call them resting cells."

"How often?"

The darkhaired android answered, "Every cell is constantly monitored electronically, Mr. Cardigan."

"But do you ever actually look inside them?"

"In the case of long-term prisoners such as Dr. Chesterton, we do that once every six months."

"When was the last check made?"

"Four and a half months ago."

"And he was there then?"

"If he hadn't been, the inspector for that tier of the penal colony would have reported it."

Jake kicked at the coffin again. "Why didn't your monitoring gear notice he wasn't inside here?"

"We're investigating that," said Silverman.

"Tampering," said one of the robots.

"How's that?" asked the deputy warden.

"A report's just coming in." The robot tapped his temple. "The monitoring equipment connected to the resting cell of Prisoner #18,977 has had a Diverter Box attached to it."

"Feeding in fake information," observed Jake, "for the last four or five months."

"This is extremely serious." Deputy Warden Silverman frowned deeply. "It's starting to sound as though this prisoner has been smuggled out of here. Something that has never happened before."

"As far as you know it's never happened before."

"We won't be needing you any longer," Silverman told him. "Should we determine the current whereabouts of Gordon Chesterton—"

"Or his remains."

"What do you mean by that?"

"Several people who were associated with Chesterton down on Earth have died lately," Jake said. "It could be that somebody wants him dead, too."

"But the man was as good as dead already. Fifty years up here is a long time."

"Yeah, but it's not quite as permanent as death." Jake headed for the doorway, where the robot who'd brought him was waiting.

"It goes without saying, that if you find out anything about what's become of Chesterton," said the deputy warden, "that you inform us at once."

"I'll tell Cosmos, they'll tell you."

Jake and the robot started along a grey corridor. Just around the first bend a wall panel slid quietly open on his right.

"Jake," called a faint voice, "I think I can help you."

■

Killcrazy Maisie had straightarmed the first guard.

He went skittering backwards, dropping his stunrifle on the ribbed walkway and slamming into a metal wall.

Moonbase Minnie had, meantime, grabbed the second and third guards at the private docking area and bonged their heads together.

"That's not fair, honey," complained Tessie the Torpedo. "You didn't leave any of them for me."

"Onward," urged Gomez, stepping over one of the unconscious guards.

He and Natalie ran out into the glasswalled docking area. There were three silvery shuttles resting there in launching cradles.

Gomez consulted the key he'd borrowed from the slumbering Leon. "We're seeking FSG/3," he said, scanning the row of shuttles. "Ah, *aquí.*" He realized that he was standing beside the spacecraft he wanted.

"We've really appreciated your help," Natalie told the trio of android lady wrestlers. "I hope that by aiding us you won't find yourselves in any trouble with the slugs who manage this—"

"Horsepuckey, sweetie," cut in Tessie. "Save your goodbyes, because we're fixing to go with you."

"But that wouldn't be—"

"Arguing slows down our departure." Gomez unlocked the cabin and climbed aboard.

"But, Gomez, I don't really think we can steal three androids right out from under—"

"We're already stealing this shuttle." He settled, after bouncing a few times, into the pilot seat.

"Actually I look on it more as borrowing, since once we've reached GLA, we can arrange to have—"

"Nat, seat yourself next to me and buckle yourself in," he told her. "Tessie, you and your sisters hop aboard and get ready. We've got to exit *muy rápidamente.*"

"Right you are, cutie."

In less than three minutes everyone was safely aboard. In less than six minutes the shuttle was roaring away from The Casino.

⣞23⣏

or nearly half a minute, Jake didn't recognize the person who had called to him.

Just beyond the opening that had appeared in the wall sat a frail, gaunt man in a dark metal servochair. The thin hands that clutched the arms of the wheeled chair were almost skeletal, his skin was grey. "How're you doing, Jake?" he asked in a dim, tired voice.

Jake took a few steps closer. "Pete Goodhill?"

"You haven't seen me for a while," said the frail Goodhill.

"Not since I checked into the Freezer four years ago. Are you still the prison psychiatrist?"

The doctor's mouth twisted into something that might have been a smile. "Until they can replace me."

"What exactly is—"

"A rare sort of malignancy is what's killing me. One, unfortunately, there's still no cure for."

Jake's robot guide said, "They'll be expecting us, sir, back in the Administration—"

Dr. Goodhill had touched one of the buttons on the left arm of his chair. A thin sizzling beam of orange light shot out of a small nozzle on the side of the chair. It hit the robot in the chest.

With a rattling gasp, the mechanical man's eyes snapped shut, his arms dropped to his sides and he stood rigid.

"Come in here for a while, Jake. I need to talk to you."

Glancing at the incapacitated robot, Jake stepped through the wall. "Still not getting along with your colleagues, Pete," he observed. "Same way you were when you worked with the SoCal State Police."

"Back then I didn't have to rely on a damn chair to take care of the assholes who annoyed me." Goodhill's chair rolled across the small room that was behind the wall and out into another corridor. "Just down this way. Excuse, by the way, my showing selfpity a moment ago. Bad thing for a psychiatrist to do, not a good example for his patients. Dying, though, can really depress the hell out of you when you get to thinking about it. Anyway, Jake, I'm glad you finally got out of this place. I was sure all along that you'd been framed."

"I know, Pete. A few other people were, too, but nobody could prove it."

A white door opened on their right. "My office." The servochair carried the frail, dying man across the threshold of a large room with bright orange and yellow walls. "I had my chair do a little decorating for me. Warm colors, I find, cheer me up."

"This colony isn't noted for being a warm place." Jake sat in a crimson chair. "Sometimes I think . . ."

"Think what, Jake?"

"I don't know, Pete. That I was actually frozen while I was up here and that I still haven't completely thawed out."

Goodhill touched another button on the chair arm. A thin silvery rod popped out of the chair, snaked up and wiped his nose with a plyochief. "The aftereffects of a stay in the Freezer have never been adequately studied. I've been planning a book that will . . . Shit, what am I saying? I won't be around long enough for that."

"Isn't there anything that might—"

"No, nope. This isn't Chesterton's virus, Jake. There's no cure."

"You know about Chesterton?"

"I know what you've been working on."

"Any idea who swiped his body?"

Goodhill touched a button on the right arm of the chair. Another metal rod swung up, this one pressing a small oxygen mask to his face. When it retracted, he said, "I don't have any concrete evidence of this, Jake, yet I know I'm right." A wheeze sounded in his thin voice. "What you have to do if you want to locate Gordon Chesterton is talk to the warden."

"Warden Niewenhaus?"

"Yeah, him. You won't find him aboard the Freezer. He's most likely at home, down in the Malibu Sector of GLA. The prison makes him uneasy, all these poor bastards sleeping here. 'They're like deadmen, Peter,'" said Dr. Goodhill. "Since I'm just about a deadman myself, I probably scare him, too. Forgive me—more selfpity."

"I've been accused of that myself lately," said Jake. "Must be a lot of it going around."

"Having a rough time down there?"

"You heard about my exwife?"

"She's got the plague."

"Somehow Dan, my son, thinks that I—"

"I know Dan. Remember, I was at his tenth birthday party?"

"Right, you did your magic act for them. Dan really . . ." Jake trailed off.

"It's all right, Jake. It doesn't bother me to be reminded that I can't even blow my own nose anymore, let alone pull gold coins out of a kid's ear."

All at once Jake's head went forward. Bringing his hand up to his face, he started crying. It only lasted a few seconds. Then he took a deep breath, shaking his head. "Why the hell did I do that?"

"Well, it might be you're sad at seeing me in this shape," said the psychiatrist. "And it also might be that you're starting to thaw a little more." Goodhill touched the chair arm and the door to his office slid open. "I better escort you back to your custodian now. No use having them come hunting for us."

Standing, Jake said, "Thanks for the tip about the warden."

"I've suspected for quite a while, Jake, that he's arranged for a few choice prisoners to take unauthorized leave. Chesterton is sure to be one of them."

As Goodhill rolled by him, Jake reached out to pat the ailing doctor's shoulder. "Good luck, Pete."

"You're developing a sentimental side." Goodhill's chair took him out into the corridor. "Bothering to wish good luck to a deadman."

■

Onita Mixon came striding toward him across the Administration Office. "Damn it, you were supposed to send for me soon as Chesterton woke up." She halted a foot from him, glaring.

"At the moment, Nita, nobody's certain if he's awake or asleep."

"If you went ahead and questioned him without . . . What the hell are you talking about?"

Backing off from her, he answered, "Dr. Chesterton wasn't in his coffin."

"Where is he?"

"That's what a lot of people—and mechanisms—hereabouts are trying to find out."

The National Disease Control Agency agent, turning her back on Jake, walked over to the desk. "Why didn't you tell me about this when I was asking you what was delaying Cardigan?"

"Because, ma'am, that would have been in violation of our security procedures," replied the voxbox.

Onita slammed a fist on the desk top. "Security, my fanny! This is an important government investigation," she said. "I want to talk to the warden. Right now!"

"He's not available at this time."

Beth moved up close beside Jake. "Is he really missing?"

"That he is."

"Any idea where to find him?"

"Yep." In a louder voice he said, "Since we've hit a dead end, we'd like to take the next shuttle home."

"One will be leaving in seventeen and a half minutes," the desk informed him. "Is the entire party intending to—"

"I'm staying here until I find out what's been done with Dr. Chesterton." Spinning, Onita came back across to scowl at Jake. "Do you know anything about what happened?"

"That's what the deputy warden was just asking me," he said. "The answer I gave him was—nope, nothing."

"I think maybe you do, though." She raised her right hand, about to prod him in the chest.

"Didn't I mention," said Beth, grabbing her wrist, "that you were really starting to annoy me?" Using the angry agent's arm as a lever, she flipped her aside.

Onita stumbled, fell to the floor.

One of her robot associates trotted over to help her up, the other closed in on Beth.

Jake stepped in front of the young woman, holding up his hand. "The fracas is over," he said warningly to the whitecoated robot. "You don't want to risk any danger to your own person."

Getting up, Onita ordered, "Lay off them, Ernie."

"But they—"

"Later," she promised, brushing at her skirt. "I'll get even later."

"Be looking forward to that." Grinning, Jake escorted Beth out of the room.

⠅24⠅

There were five other passengers on the homeward-bound shuttle, not counting Agent MacQuarrie.

Across the aisle from Beth and Jake a heavyset blonde woman was crying quietly. "Fifteen years," she was saying again. "That's such a long time."

"No, it's not really," said the slender blonde teenage girl sitting with her. "And Dad's already been there for two."

"I'm going to be sixty-one when they let him out."

"That's not old, not terribly old anyway."

"But he'll still be forty-seven." She shook her head. "I don't know why we go up there once a month, just to look at a vidpicture of him lying in that awful cramped box."

"It does you good, Ma."

"Does it? Fifteen years."

Jake said quietly, "A sad place."

"You got through the visit all right." Beth took hold of his hand.

"Not exactly." He told her about his encounter with the dying Dr. Goodhill, about breaking down and crying.

Beth asked, "Were you crying for him?"

"Partly," he answered. "But partly for Kate, partly for Dan . . . and maybe for myself, too."

"It could be Goodhill was right and you're warming up, Jake," said Beth. "That seems to bother you, though, doesn't it? Having feelings, being vulnerable."

"When I was a cop, they called me—although I wasn't supposed to know it—Andy. Short for android." He leaned back in the seat, holding her hand tighter. "My father wasn't exactly a warm person."

"So I've gathered," she said. "Do you think Warden Niewenhaus is really involved in whatever happened to Chesterton?"

"Pete Goodhill thinks so."

"Were you close friends when you were both with the State Police?"

"Not exactly. It was more like we were eventually going to get around to being friends but never quite did. I trust him, though."

The heavyset woman across the aisle was asking him something.

"I didn't catch that," said Jake.

"I was wondering if you'd been visiting someone on the Freezer," she said, wiping her eyes.

"In a way, yes."

"Who—a relative?"

"Me," answered Jake.

■

They caught Jake in the middle of the main building of the Oakland Spaceport.

The big chromeplated robot spotted him first and, turning the vidcam mounted in his gleaming skull toward him, came rolling over. "Are you investigating the plague, too, Jake?" the Timelife Media robot asked.

Jake, with Beth close beside him and Agent MacQuarrie trailing, had been heading toward a bank of vidphones. He wanted to make a call to the Marina Hospital. "What plague, Scoop?" he asked, halting.

Three human reporters joined the Timelife robot. Pachter of Newz, Inc., Gary Insatsu of the Japanese Shinbun Vidnews Service and a silverhaired young woman Jake didn't recognize.

"Quit shamming, Jake," said Pachter, a lean dark man of forty.

"You know all about the vicious blight that's laying waste to San Francisco, turning the once-glittering city into a pesthole where death holds sway and—"

"Christ, Pach," cut in the silverhaired woman, "write your story on your own time, huh? Why were you up on the Freezer, Cardigan? Did you go along with Agent Mixon?"

"What do you think about the plans to quarantine Frisco?" asked Insatsu. "Do you feel, knowing what you know, that such a move is justified?"

"Folks." Jake held up his hand in a stop-right-there gesture. "I was simply visiting a friend of mine who's ailing."

"And it's just a coincidence that Mixon, who's investigating the plague, was on the same shuttle you took up there?" asked the woman.

"That's right."

"She didn't return with you, though," said Pachter. "Does that indicate she's pursuing some further link between this dreadful blight and the criminals who are incarcerated within the unyielding metal walls of—"

"You want to find out what Nita's up to, Pach, you ask her." Jake took hold of Beth's arm. "Right now I have to—"

"We've been waiting for Agent Mixon for near an hour," said Insatsu. "Word was she'd be coming home on the same ship with you."

"She didn't." Jake started walking again.

"Your own wife lies dying, a victim of this horrible and deadly scourge." Pachter walked along beside them. "Yet you seem to be exhibiting little outward grief and, indeed, here you are squiring an attractive young woman other than—"

"Pach, go away," suggested Jake quietly. "Your getting socked in the nose isn't news anymore, but it's close to happening again anyway."

The silverhaired reporter was trailing them, too. "Did you divorce your wife before or after she was felled by the plague?"

Beth smiled sweetly over her shoulder. "I take care of punching all the female newshounds," she said. "Shoo."

"It would be best, Jake," said Insatsu, catching up with him, "for you to cooperate with us. This is too big a story to keep quiet any longer. If you help us out, we'll help you."

Jake stopped again. "I'm just an operative with the Cosmos Detective Agency these days," he said, "and I'm working on a case. When I heard that an old police colleague of mine was sick, I took time off to visit him. That's all I have to say."

Pachter warned, "You'd be welladvised, Jake, to deal honestly and truthfully with us."

"I am." He started for a doorway out. "The interview is over."

"For now." Pachter didn't bother to follow him any further.

The other newspeople gave up, too. Jake and Beth stepped out into the twilight.

"A shame the story got out," he said.

"That was inevitable."

"Too damn many things are."

■

The skycar sped southward through the dusk. Beth was in the pilot seat, Jake sat next to her using the vidphone that was built into the dash.

"Marina Hospital," he was explaining to the grey robot who showed on the small phone screen.

"I'm sorry, sir, we're unable to place that call."

"Why?"

"A state order, issued three hours and seventeen minutes ago, forbids any but emergency communications with all San Francisco-area hospitals."

"This is an emergency. My former wife is a patient."

"We're in the process of setting up a special information number, sir. Once that's in place, you'll be able to—"

"My son's there, too, but only for observation. Can you put me through to him?"

"I'm sorry, sir, but the same restrictions apply."

"Okay, thanks." He blanked the screen, sank back in his seat. "Well, I better start pulling strings so I can override this—"

The phone buzzed.

Jake answered it. "Dan," he said when his son's image flashed onto the screen. "I've been trying to reach you."

"I don't have much time," said his son. "We're not supposed to make any calls out of here, but a nurse who's a friend of mine—"

"How are you?"

"I'm okay I guess. They tested me again this afternoon and everything was fine," answered Dan. "But I'm going to have to stay here anyway. They won't let anyone who's in the hospital now get out. And you can't come in to see me either."

"What about your mother?"

"They told me she's about the same," said Dan. "Dad, listen. I saw you on the vidnews a little while ago, so I knew you were back. It said you'd been up to the Freezer and that it must have something to do with the plague. I was hoping that you'd found out something. You know, that you'd found out some way to cure the plague."

"I know what's causing it and, in general, who's probably behind it."

"But can't you tell them how to save Mom?"

"Not yet, no." Jake shook his head. "But I'm getting closer."

"I don't think there's too much more time to—"

The screen suddenly went blank.

"Damn," said Jake. "They cut him off."

Beth said, "Sounds like he's thawing some, too."

"It does, yeah," admitted Jake. "But, as far as he's concerned, I'm still letting him down."

⚏25⚏

"Don't," advised Jake.

Warden Niewenhaus's right hand slowed, stopped in midair over the Lucite table beside the deep nearleather armchair he was sitting in. A black lazgun rested on the tabletop, barrel touching an ivory ball-clock. "This is a very serious matter, coming into my home and threatening me with a gun."

Jake grinned, keeping his stungun aimed at the tall, thickset man. "Let's chat about Gordon Chesterton."

The warden dropped his hand to his knee. "You're Cardigan—the one who was up at the Freezer earlier today making trouble." He glanced around his large study, his frown deepening.

A large single plastiglass window filled the far wall, giving a wide view of the moonlit Pacific directly below. The house was built on stilts out over the ocean and bordering the window was a narrow deck.

Jake asked, "Where's Chesterton?"

"I don't know how you sneaked by my security robots, but they'll be coming in here soon, Cardigan, damn soon to haul you off. Then, I'm afraid, it'll be another stretch in the Freezer for you."

"Your security bots, all three of them, are incapacitated." Jake sat on the arm of a low white sofa. "Something I learned how to do in my police days. Now about—"

"I might as well warn you that I have a very efficient electronic alarm system. As soon as you walked in, it—"

"I incapacitated that, too."

"Then I've got no security here at all." He started to stand. "It's not safe to stay in—"

"Keep in the chair."

"You damned idiot. Now they can get in, too."

"Somebody the Teklords are sending around?"

"I have absolutely no connection with—"

"Nobody was supposed to find out that Chesterton wasn't still up there. A fifty-year sentence with no possibility of parole—who'd miss him?" Jake settled down on the sofa. "The efficient thing for the Teklords to do now is to knock you off. So you can't tell anybody where Chesterton went."

"Cardigan, I don't intend to discuss—"

"One way or the other you're going to tell me where he is, Warden."

The warden sagged, running his tongue over his upper lip. "They pressured me into doing it, you understand. Made threats against me and my family."

"They also paid you two million dollars."

"How did you—"

"You weren't as careful in banking the dough as you should have been. Who paid you?"

Warden Niewenhaus leaned forward, his hands pressing his knees. "Can you help me to get clear of here—to someplace safe?" he asked. "I've been fearful all day, ever since I learned that Chesterton's disappearance had been discovered."

Nodding, Jake told him, "The Cosmos Detective Agency is good at hiding people."

"I've never done anything like this before. It's the first time I ever betrayed my trust or compromised my—"

"Save that, Warden. I've been over your secret bank accounts for the past five years."

"All right," he said wearily, "all right."

"Who?"

"I never dealt with them directly. I was contacted rather by their representative, a man who arranges things for them."

"The same arranger you'd dealt with previously?"

"They've used him once or twice in the past."

"They being the Teklords?"

Warden Niewenhaus nodded slowly. "That's been my assumption."

"Who's your contact?"

"His name is Frank Holz."

"Holz?" Jake eyed the nervous man. "Frank Holz is a second-rate pornmovie producer out in the Palm Springs Sector."

"Apparently there are some things you don't know after all, Cardigan," said the warden. "Holz works for them."

"Where did he arrange to have Chesterton sent?"

"I don't know."

"Make a guess."

"I really have no—"

"Guess anyway."

"Possibly Japan."

"Why Japan?"

"I've heard that . . . that certain people associated with the Hokori cartel had an interest in Dr. Chesterton."

"Any names?"

"No." He shook his head negatively several times, in a quick jerky way.

"Have you figured out what they're using Chesterton for?"

"What happens after a prisoner leaves the Freezer isn't any concern of—"

"The plague. The one that's killing people up in San Francisco is his invention."

"I don't believe that at all. I certainly wouldn't have been a party to this had I known that—"

"C'mon, for two million bucks you'd be a party to anything. How long ago was Chesterton smuggled out of the Freezer?"

"It's been approximately three months."

"Then Sonny Hokori was still alive when the deal was set up."

"Yes, and you were still one of my guests in the Freezer. I wish you still were."

"Yeah, I imagine you do," said Jake. "Now, suppose you tell me—"

Just then the entire viewindow shattered and hundreds of glittering fragments of jagged glass exploded into the room.

■

Gomez whistled as he flew.

He was piloting an agency skycar through the night, heading for the Malibu Sector of Greater Los Angeles. Fresh back from his excursion to The Casino and no longer encumbered with a redhaired reporter or mechanical wrestlers, he was aiming to catch up with Jake.

When Bascom at the Cosmos Agency told him where his partner was heading, Gomez decided Jake might be in need of some backup help tonight.

On the small vidscreen mounted on the dash a wavyhaired android newscaster was droning. "Just in from San Francisco. As the number of plague cases grows at an alarming rate in the city by the bay, state and national officials continue to deny that the virus ravaging the city is a spillover from a secret military experiment gone awry. NorCal Governor Vetterlein alleged earlier in the day, at a hastily called news conference in the State House in Alameda, that the manmade plague is the work of terrorists. He could not, however, when pressed for details by reporters, name the specific terrorist group responsible. Meantime, all public and private schools in San Francisco were ordered closed until—"

"Muy malo," commented Gomez as he turned off the screen.

The Malibu Sector coastline, outlined by scatters of lights, was coming up below him.

"How close are we to the warden's *casa?"* he asked the control panel.

"Two miles," replied the voxbox. "We'll be over it in a few secs."

Dropping down a thousand feet, Gomez put the skycar into a slow circling pattern.

He passed fairly close to a speeding pizza-delivery skyvan. The startled driver threw him the finger.

Gomez merely smiled.

"Niewenhaus place directly below," announced the voxbox, turning on the vidscreen to show him a nightcam picture of the stilt-house. "It's the one where those three masked figures are climbing up out of the sea and onto the deck."

"*¡Caramba!*" remarked Gomez.

As he watched, the third and last of the intruders reached the deck of the prison official's house.

Seconds later the viewindow exploded and the three dark figures went diving into the house in the wake of the flying fragments of shattered plastiglass.

"Shit, if Jake's paying a social call in there," said Gomez, dropping close to the besieged waterside house, "he's liable to get sliced up."

Out of the gap a dark figure came sailing. It was one of the raiders and, judging by the way he flipped over the deck railing and dropped into the sea, he was out cold.

Next came Jake, executing a neat dive and hitting the water with a foamy splash.

Swooping lower, Gomez instructed the skycar, "Stungun anybody else who pops out of that joint down there."

"Right you are."

His aircar skimmed the water, started hovering near the spot where Jake had gone in.

"Bingo," said the voxbox. "We got one."

"*Bueno.*" Gomez touched a key on the control panel and a door opened in the belly of the hovering car. "Jake, unless you need the exercise, you can quit swimming now and climb aboard," he shouted down at the dark water.

Jake's head showed above the surface. He blinked, spit out water, grinned. "You're back, huh?"

"Apparently, *amigo.*" He touched another key and a ladder unfurled.

The skycar was hovering about five feet above the ocean.

Using the dangling ladder, Jake climbed up inside the aircar. Dripping and soggy, he crossed and slumped into a seat. "Thanks, Sid."

"*Por nada.* All part of our friendly service." He set the car to climbing away from there. "Was the warden at home?"

"He was, but the shattering glass killed him." Jake tugged out a damp plyochief and touched at a curved, bleeding cut on his cheek. "I hit the floor and missed getting sliced up. Doing okay with those housebreakers who came in by way of the deck, but—"

"I noted one of them doing some impromptu water ballet work thanks to you."

"Yeah, and I downed a second one. But then five more of them came in through the front door."

"A good time to make an exit."

"That's what I decided."

"Did you get any answers out of the good warden before the intrusion?"

"Yes, and I think we better head for the Palm Springs Sector right now."

"Which part—the Dirty Hollywood area?"

"Yeah," answered Jake, "that's exactly where we have to go."

"One of the scenic wonders of Greater LA," observed his partner.

⋮26⋮

Gomez headed the skycar inland through the night. "How's Kate doing?"

"No better." Jake had taken off his wet jacket, shirt and trousers and had them spread out on the cabin floor next to an aircirc outlet to dry. He was crouched on the floor near the clothes. "Dan is fine, though. He doesn't have it, but they're keeping him in the hospital."

Nodding, his partner said, "Bascom filled me in on what you've dug up on Chesterton. Did the warden really arrange for his premature departure from the Freezer?"

"Yeah, Chesterton was turned over to Frank Holz."

"Ah, the porn entrepreneur. I always figured Frank was tied in with the Tek bunch."

"Niewenhaus was pretty sure the Hokori cartel was involved. Chesterton was smuggled out before Sonny got killed."

Gomez said, "It looks like there's still a Hokori cartel flourishing, *amigo*. Judging from what I chanced to overhear up at The Casino, Tora Hokori is trying to run this whole show."

"That's the *late* Tora Hokori?"

"The lady is still above the ground—or at least several fairly astute Teklords sure think so." Gomez went on to tell Jake about his activities aboard the gambling satellite and what he'd been able to learn.

"So the Teklords are definitely behind the plague," said Jake when his partner had concluded.

"*Sí*, it's basically an extortion operation. Lay off us or we'll wipe out a few choice cities—commencing with Frisco."

"What about an antidote?"

"We were interrupted before there was much discussion of that. But obviously the antidote is what they intend to sell."

Jake poked at his trousers. "Dry enough," he decided, starting to pull them on. "What'd you end up doing with your lady wrestlers?"

"Sent the trio down to a chum of mine who runs a sports pavilion in the San Pedro Sector. He's a chap who's not too fastidious about the pedigrees of andies."

"And Natalie Dent?"

"Not being able to think of a place to ship her to, I simply snuck away soon as we landed in Greater LA," he said.

Jake put on his shirt. "What I'm worried about now is time," he said. "If we don't find Chesterton soon, it's going to be too late to help Kate."

"We'll track him down."

"If she dies . . ." He didn't finish the sentence. "Hell, I don't even know what I feel about her. It's as though I didn't come back to the same world after I got out of the damn Freezer. Everything had changed—Kate didn't really love me, she'd helped set me up."

"Could be, Jake, the world didn't change that much in your absence. You just started seeing it a mite more clearly."

Jake got into his jacket. "But, Sid, I should've seen what was going on before I ever let them frame me."

"You didn't and that's all over and done," said Gomez. "Keep in mind, however, that I have remained consistent. A tower of strength in the midst of turmoil, a beacon blazing steadfastly in the stormy sea of change, a refuge in the dark night of the soul as well as—"

"A prime example of modesty." Jake grinned. "Okay, I'll quit complaining."

His partner announced, "And there's our glittering destination now!"

■

Dirty Hollywood occupied seven square blocks at the south end of the Palm Springs Sector. Seven square blocks devoted to the production and distribution of pornographic entertainment and allied arts. The glare of the neon signs and the gloletters was formidable. Jake and Gomez, on foot now, passed beneath the huge glittering arch that proclaimed DIRTY HOLLYWOOD—PORN CAPITAL OF THE WORLD! and started along the main thoroughfare.

The light signs glared and flashed all around them—TORRID FILMS, LTD.; HOTZ BROS. BOOKZ; PRINTED PORN FOR THE COLLECTOR; PANSY'S GAY PORN EMPORIUM; SEXY LEXY'S PORN SUPERMARKET—5 FLOORS OF FILTH!; FOULMOUTH FREDDIE'S PHONESEX PARLOR— COME IN & TALK DIRTY; SMUTZ' DINER.

"We want the diner." Dodging tourists, Gomez went ducking through the entryway.

The place was built to resemble a middle-twentieth-century diner. Long and narrow, it had a counter running along one side and a row of booths along the other. Most of the booths were occupied.

Gomez went over to the counter. "I used to know a lovely young lady who worked here in Dirty Hollywood," he told Jake, perching on the edge of a stool and scanning the room. "Very pretty auburn-haired lass named Teena who was, unfortunately, starring in some of Frank Holz's epics. If I can find her, she can provide us with some tips on how we can unobtrusively contact the gent."

"She hangs out here?"

"Used to."

A plump, puffyfaced woman with bright carrot-colored hair was sitting two stools over. She had both shabby elbows resting on the countertop, her hands clutching her mug of nearcaf. "Who you looking for?"

Gomez continued to look around. "Just a friend of mine."

The plump woman straightened up, brushing at her hair. "Holy Ghost, it is you, isn't it?" She reached over, took hold of his wrist. "Gomez, how are you?"

"Madre. Is that you, Teena?"

She smiled. "I've put on a little weight these past couple years."

"A little," he agreed.

"Why're you looking for me?"

"I'm seeking information, Teena."

Carefully, she gathered up her cup and moved over to sit next to him. "I'd like to help you, Gomez. But . . . is there any dough involved?"

"Sure. Let us buy you dinner and we'll talk."

She shook her head. "I don't want to be seen talking too long in public with a cop."

"I'm not a cop anymore."

"But you're still some kind of detective."

"Private. This is my partner, Jake Cardigan."

"He used to be a cop, too."

"That's right," said Jake. "Where can we get together with you?"

"My place in about fifteen minutes."

"Are you still living in the château out on—"

"No," said Teena, laughing. "I've got a room out back of McSeedy's. It's 101A."

"Okay, Teena." Gomez started to get up.

She caught his arm. "Is the money going to be maybe as much as five hundred dollars?"

He smiled. "At least, *chiquita.*"

⠿27⠿

rank Holz was having a party.

It was being held, with well over a hundred guests in attendance, at his home on the edge of the Palm Springs Sector. The home had once been the area's leading motel and when it was converted to a private residence, the huge glosign proclaiming GOLDEN OASIS INN had been left in place over the high silverplated entrance gates.

Jake and Gomez arrived there about a half hour shy of midnight. Gomez, smiling broadly at the tuxedoed chrome robot overseeing the gates, handed him the plascard invitation that Teena had obtained for them. "*Aquí,*" he said. "I trust we're not too late for the festivities."

"The night's young, gents, the party's still in full flower." The robot touched the invitation to his forehead, causing his left eye to flash green. "Go on in, gents, you're legit."

"Get many crashers?" inquired Jake as the silvery gates clicked open.

"A few try, but Mr. Holz's goon squad gives them the bum's rush. Enjoy yourselves, gents."

When they were safely in the party area around the large outdoor swimming pool, Gomez said, "Remind me to avoid that goon squad."

A large, wide bandstand hovered three feet from the ground just beyond the shimmering pale-green pool. A full android band, decked out in tuxedos, was playing antique dance music. A large glosign affixed to the hovering stand announced—GUY LOMBARDO & HIS ROYAL CANADIENS. AN AUTHENTIC 20TH CENTURY ORCHESTRA RE-CREATED FOR YOUR DANCING PLEASURE BY MUSIKANDIES, INC.

"Do you know what it costs Frank to rent that band for just one night?" a lovely blonde was asking her thickset escort.

"Too much," he grunted.

Gomez and Jake halted near a wheeled robot bartender and studied the crowd of party guests.

"There's Holz over yonder," said Jake quietly. "To the left of the bandstand."

"Chatting with a gaggle of his porn distributors I'd guess."

Holz was a slim pale man with a minimum of hair and a thin moustache. Circling him were four hefty men, three of whom were bald. The one with hair had a three-foot-high calculator robot in tow and the squat mechanism was chuffing out a ribbon of plazpaper covered with figures from a slot in its metal chest.

"Business," observed Gomez, "always business."

"Let's go over and talk some business to Holz ourselves."

"Jake! Love!" A very tall blonde young woman had pushed her way through a group of poolside guests. She was wearing a scanty crimson dress trimmed in neon. Putting both arms tight around Jake, she kissed him full on the mouth, then patted his backside with her left hand. "Gee, I was under the impression you were still up in the cooler."

Jake, gently, broke her hold. "Camilla," he said, grinning, "would you do me a favor? Don't holler my name hereabouts."

The pretty blonde winked and lowered her voice. "You're here undercover, huh?" She laughed, knuckling his ribs fondly with her fist. "I get the picture. Who's your colleague?"

"I'm Gomez," explained Gomez. "You're Camilla Jugend, aren't you?"

She smiled, reaching out to rumple his hair. "The Porn Queen, that's me. We've got three vidcazes on the charts this week. Haven't hit the top spot with any of them yet, but I'm in three, six and eight.

Not bad for a onetime street hooker from the Santa Monica Sector."

"It's the American dream in action," agreed Gomez.

Camilla gave Jake another hug. "Gee, I heard you got sent up to the darn Freezer for life or something."

"That turned out to be a mistake," he told her. "Camilla, could you introduce us to Holz and give him the impression we're starting up a porn distribution system in—"

"In Central America," suggested Gomez. "Since I'm often mistaken for a Central American business tycoon."

Camilla asked, "You aren't planning to arrest Frank, are you?"

"Nope. We're not cops anymore."

"What then?"

"Operatives with Cosmos," he replied. "We don't intend to do him any serious harm. Only interested in asking a few questions."

"Oh, hey, listen, if you roughed him up a little it wouldn't annoy me much," said the blonde actress. "But were you to haul him away to the pokey, that might affect the Cultural Productions, Inc., studios—that's what Frank's calling himself—and that in turn would futz up my still-burgeoning career." She smiled at Gomez. "How many of my films have you seen?"

"One."

"Oh, so? How many times did you watch it?"

"Once."

"Really? What was wrong with it?"

"Not a blessed thing, but—"

"Camilla," persisted Jake, "what about the introduction?"

"Sure, I can do that much for an old friend from my former life," she assured him. "Who are you supposed to be?"

"I'm Mr. Jaxon, he's Mr. Chavez."

Camilla studied Gomez. "No, he doesn't look like a Chavez to me," she decided. "We'll call him Mr. McTavish."

"That's not," Gomez pointed out, "an especially apt name for a Central American tycoon, Camilla."

"But it suits you." She took hold of his hand. "Come along, Mr. McTavish. You, too, Mr. Jaxon." She caught hold of Jake's hand. "We'll go meet Mr. Holz."

.

Holz settled into his desk chair. "If you find the wall distracting, gentlemen," he said, chuckling, "I can switch it off."

They were in his den, which had formerly been the office of the Golden Oasis Inn. On the wall behind the desk were five rows of a dozen vidscreens each.

"Are those samples of your wares?" Jake was sitting in a rubberoid chair facing the desk. To his right was a door leading to what had once been the motel parking lot.

Chuckling again, Holz traced his moustache with the tip of his little finger. "What you're seeing, gentlemen, is what's going on in the bedrooms right now. I've got fifty-seven bedrooms in my mansion, each one monitored." He pointed to a screen. "There, for instance, is Mayor Merner in bed with one of her constituents. Up on Screen 13 you see Romo Styx—actually it's his number one andy simulacrum, but she doesn't know that—making love to a reporter from *Porn-Billboard.*"

"Interesting," commented Gomez, who was seated near the door to the pool area. "But, as you mentioned, a mite distracting during a business conference."

Holz touched a key pad on the left side of his desk. All sixty screens died. "When do you intend to begin operations, Mr. McTavish? That's an odd name, if you don't mind my saying so, for a Central American."

"I'm the product of a mixed marriage."

Jake said, "What I'd like you to do now, Holz, is fold your hands and keep them in your lap."

"Huh? What the hell do you—"

"Do it."

Gomez, swiftly, produced a lazgun. "All we want is a small amount of information."

"McTavish, you may not be aware of this, but I happen to be in partnership with some very powerful people," warned the pornographer. "You really don't want to antagonize any of the—"

"It's your partners we're interested in." Standing up, Jake drew his stungun. "You arranged with Warden Niewenhaus to get Dr. Gordon Chesterton off the Freezer."

"That's absolute bullshit. I never had—"

"This isn't a debate," Jake said. "I'm just telling you what happened."

"Yeah? Well, I'm telling you that if you mess with me you're going to have a half dozen Teklords on your ass."

"That's probable, sure," said Jake. "But by that time you'll be in less than tip-top shape. Unless you cooperate."

"Who're you with—one of the drug agencies?"

"Where'd you send Chesterton?" Jake moved over beside the seated man. "You can't seriously injure a man with a stungun like this—unless you use it in an unconventional way."

"As a bludgeon, for example," suggested Gomez.

Holz said, "Both you assholes are going to be dead in a very—"

"In the meantime—tell us where Chesterton is."

"I don't know."

Gomez sighed. "That's not a very satisfying answer, *amigo.*"

"Listen, all I did was make arrangements to spring the bastard and accept delivery."

"Had Chesterton been revived by the time you got him?" asked Jake.

"No, he was still in a box. I never even actually saw the guy."

"Where'd the box go?"

"I turned it over to somebody."

"Who?"

"I had the box delivered—unopened—to the Otosu Express Service in the San Pedro Sector. That was months ago and I have no idea where the goddamn thing went after that."

"Who ordered you to arrange for Chesterton's—"

A pounding began on the poolside door to the office. "Boss? You doing okay in there?"

Holz smiled. "I neglected to mention that my goon squad checks on me every ten minutes when I'm in a meeting with anybody they don't know," he said. "What shall I tell them, gentlemen?"

⠠⠃28⠠⠃

Jake said to Holz, "Tell your thugs everything is fine."

"That wouldn't be to my advantage."

"Hey, boss—shall we bust in?"

"If I don't respond at all, they'll come on in anyway." Holz chuckled. "Looks to me as though . . . Yow!"

Jake had used his stungun on him.

Holz stiffened in his chair, started to bring his hands up out of his lap. His mouth made a snapping sound as he slumped in the chair, unconscious.

Jake caught him, kept him from making a noisy fall to the floor. "Time to leave the party, Sid."

Gomez was already at the rear door to the office and opening it cautiously. "No goons out this way yet."

"Okay, boss, we're coming in. Stand clear," said one of the men at the front door.

Jake followed his partner out into the night. "Trouble," he said.

Coming around the side of the building, about a hundred yards to their left, were two large men in tight suits. Each carried a lazgun.

"We can borrow this crate," said Gomez.

Parked about fifty feet to their right was a large black skybus. Emblazoned on its side in silver gloletters was—GUY LOMBARDO & HIS ROYAL CANADIENS—ANOTHER MUSIKANDIES FAVORITE!

Jake halted, dropped to the ground and fired.

The beam of his stungun hit the first goon. The big man formed a sudden X, then crumpled and fell.

The other man fired his lazgun at Jake.

He missed, succeeded only in slicing the back door of Holz's office in half.

Rolling, Jake fired again.

He missed, too.

"Allow me." Gomez had yanked out his stungun. He brought the second thug down.

"Thanks." Rising up, Jake ran over to the bus.

Gomez had the door open. "I can fly this thing—by using a parasite control I happen to have," he said, climbing aboard.

"I won't mention to anyone that you were carrying an illegal device on your person."

"Pick a comfortable seat and let's take off." Gomez hopped into the pilot seat and slapped a small orange disk on the control panel. "I just noticed that more goons are pouring out of what used to be Holz's back door."

The skybus roared to life, its door wooshed shut.

"Muy bien." Gomez punched out a takeoff pattern. The big bus quivered, rattled once, then started climbing rapidly up into the midnight sky.

Three of Holz's crew were standing down below, firing up at the escaping skybus with lazguns.

One of them hit it and managed to cut a neat saucer-sized hole in the floor of the rapidly rising craft about five feet from where Jake was standing.

Gomez said, "That hit doesn't seem to have done us any serious harm. I think we'd better keep this crate until we're a safe distance away. Our agency car can be reclaimed at a later date."

Jake was looking down out a window. "Nobody is taking off after us."

"With Holz unable to give orders, they probably don't know whether or not to chase us. How long will he stay out cold?"

"Had my stungun on the maximum setting. So figure twelve to fifteen hours."

"Then maybe we'll have enough time to investigate the Otosu Express folks before anyone can warn them."

"Maybe," said Jake.

•

Beth said, "Dan wants to talk to you. He's phoned here several times."

It was nearly three A.M. The young woman was dressed, waiting up for him in the living room of her apartment.

Jake had just come in. "Did he say what it is?"

"He's all right. I think it has to do with Kate."

"Is she still alive?"

"Yes, but your son still isn't especially fond of me, so he wouldn't leave much of a message."

"Going to have to figure a way to get through to him, since only emergency calls can—"

"He gave me the number of that nurse who's befriended him. You can reach him through her." Beth passed him the number.

Jake sank into the phone chair, feeling suddenly weary, and punched out the number. "You okay, Beth?"

"Far as I know. How'd you get the gash on your face?"

"In the line of duty. I'll . . . Hello, this is Jake Cardigan."

A plump blonde woman in a crisp white nurse uniform had shown up on the screen. "Well, it's about time. The poor kid is very upset."

"Is he awake?"

"Certainly he's awake. If you kept decent hours, he wouldn't have to fret half the night away while—"

"Okay, I'm here now. I want to talk to him."

"You sit right where you are, Mr. Cardigan. I'll fetch the poor kid." She left the screen.

Beth stroked the back of Jake's neck. "She's not, apparently, an admirer of yours."

"I've run into several people like that tonight. At least this one's not armed."

Dan, who'd obviously been crying, was on the phonescreen. "Dad, I've been trying to call you for hours."

Beth moved silently back out of range of the phone's eye.

"Sorry, Dan. What's bothering you?"

"It's Mom. She . . . she's gotten much worse."

"What's her doctor say?"

"I haven't even been able to talk to her real doctor. But one of those asshole android medics told me—"

"Don't swear," advised the nurse from offscreen.

"It's okay, my father doesn't mind. One of the andies says she's slipped into a deep coma, Dad."

"She's still alive, though. From what I've been able to find out about this plague, she still has a good chance of being—"

"A few more days. She won't live more than two or three days longer."

"Who told you that?"

"Not any of the doctors," admitted his son. "But I've been talking to lots of relatives of victims and . . . once that deep coma starts, you usually don't live very long at all. Can you get over to the hospital now? We can sneak you in and I'd really like you to be here in case . . . you know."

"Dan, I'd like to, but I can't. I've got to go to Japan early tomorrow. We're on the trail of the cure for this damn—"

"Couldn't you stop by here first?"

"Not going to be enough time for that."

"Why is this *your* job? On the vidnews they say that all kinds of government agencies are working on finding some kind of antidote for the plague."

"We've got a strong lead to follow—It's something I have to do."

"Okay . . . I suppose I sort of see what you're saying, Dad," said his son forlornly. "But . . . I still wish you could be here for a while." Turning, shoulders slumping, he walked out of the picture.

The plump nurse reappeared, shaking her head. "Poor kid," she observed, and killed the call.

Jake stood up, facing Beth. "I can't quite get him to accept or understand what I'm doing."

"He's getting closer—be patient," she said. "What's this about Japan? Did you and Gomez get a lead?"

"As it turns out, we got a couple of them. We're leaving for Kyoto at six A.M."

"Which we—you and Gomez or you and me?"

"You and me, Beth."

"You sure you want me to come along?"

"I am, yeah." He moved close to her and took hold of her.

‖29‖

orty thousand feet in the air the skyliner was speeding toward Japan.

Beth and Jake were sharing a table in the blankwalled dining room. "Eat," she suggested.

"What?"

Smiling, she pointed at his plate. "The ritual of breakfast usually involves eating," she said. "Look at Agent MacQuarrie over at that other table. He's on his second helping of soycakes and nearham."

"MacQuarrie's getting to see a lot of the world as a result of tagging after you." Jake picked up his fork. "Berkeley, the Freezer and now Kyoto."

"And Gomez is heading for where?"

"Tokyo," answered Jake. "I would've explained all this to you in greater detail last night if you hadn't distracted me."

"Forgive me. Why Kyoto and Tokyo?"

"Frank Holz was the guy who arranged to have Dr. Chesterton smuggled free of the Freezer. Holz then arranged to have the doctor, still in a suspended state, packed in a crate and turned over to an outfit in the San Pedro Sector of GLA calling itself the Otosu Express Service."

"Did you talk to them?"

"Not directly, no," said Jake, grinning. "But last night, after Gomez and I got back from the Palm Springs Sector—I'll tell you sometime about the skybus we borrowed. Last night we used the Cosmos Agency computers and a few contacts of our own in the information-siphoning trade. We found out that Otosu had shipped out not one but two crates of the size necessary to hold Chesterton's body. Both were sent to Japan at about the same time. One to a warehouse in Kyoto, the other to a shipping firm in Tokyo. Trail ends there, since we can't find out where either of the crates went next."

Beth asked, "It's possible, isn't it, that both crates are decoys? That Chesterton never left GLA?"

"Sure, and Bascom is putting some operatives on that angle."

"You're betting on Japan, though."

"Gomez found out that Tora Hokori is still alive and based in Japan someplace. Sonny Hokori seems to be the one who originally ordered Chesterton sprung from the Freezer."

"And his sister is carrying on?"

"Seems likely."

"You'd heard she was dead."

"Supposed to have been killed in a train accident. But the Teklords, at least those who attended the get-together up on The Casino, talked about her as though she was alive and trying to run things."

"They're definitely the ones behind the plague?"

"They want the United States, and most of the other countries of the world, to quit interfering with the Tek trade. San Francisco is a sort of hostage."

"If everybody agrees to lay off, then they'll hand over the antidote?"

"That seems to be the plan."

"Thousands of people are going to die before that happens."

"Which is also part of the plan."

"And if the government doesn't concede?"

"More cities."

Beth shook her head. "You can't control a plague like this one. It's going to keep spreading, beyond San Francisco and eventually beyond NorCal," she said. "They really don't know what they've turned loose, Jake."

"They don't much care. To them this is simply another useful business technique."

"If only my father hadn't . . . His anti-Tek system could've put them all out of business."

"It still may, but right now we have to stop the plague."

Beth asked, "Do you have contacts in Kyoto?"

"A few," he said. "And Bascom's arranged for me to work with an agency they've used before. An operative named Norman Itoko of the Senuku Detective Agency is going to meet us at the airport."

"There are a few people, mostly scientists, I know in Japan. I'll get in touch with them, too," she said. "You still haven't eaten anything."

"I haven't," he agreed.

■

Gomez was underwater, deep under the sea rushing toward Tokyo on one of the highspeed TransPacific Tunnel trains. The nonstop trip took just under ten hours and toward the end of the second hour he started to feel restless.

Though his compartment replicated exactly the atmosphere of life above the water, he couldn't keep from thinking about the fact that tons of ocean were pressing down on him.

The faxbook printer in his First Class compartment offered a list of twenty bestsellers. Not one of them sounded interesting. The vidwall was ready to show him any one of fifteen current hit movies. He'd already seen fourteen of them and had shunned the fifteenth.

"I'd hate to be caught watching that turkey if the Pacific broke through and flooded the train. That's not what I want to be doing during my last moments on Earth."

He got up, opened the door and went into the corridor. The train shot along the tunnel silently and with no indication of movement at all. That was one of the things about it that annoyed Gomez.

He strolled along, glancing up at the pale blue ceiling now and then.

A robot was playing romantic tunes on a chromeplated electric piano in the cocktail lounge. For some reason most of the patrons were seven- and eight-year-old children. There was at least a dozen of them scattered around at several tables, drinking soft drinks out of cocktail glasses and carrying on loud, intricate conversations between tables.

Gomez continued on into the dining car.

The smiling blond android in the pale blue suit greeted him, "Joining us again, are you, sir?"

"That's right," remembered Gomez. "I just had breakfast a half hour ago, didn't I?"

"Twenty minutes ago actually. But it's very easy to lose track of time on one of these tunnel trains."

"I'll come back later."

"We won't start serving lunch for another two hours, sir."

"Well, that gives me something to look forward to." Gomez went back through the cocktail lounge, dodging a lemon slice one of the kids tossed at another. He started along the corridor toward his compartment.

Halfway there he heard a woman in one of the other compartments cry out, faintly, "Help."

"Bueno," he told himself. "This might liven things up."

Then he recognized the voice.

⠰30⠆

omez knocked again, more forcefully, on the compartment door. "Do hurry and answer, miss," he said loudly in a voice he hoped would pass for that of an amiable android. "I have an awful lot of passengers to call on."

A few more seconds passed. Then a gruff male voice on the other side of the door suggested, "Scram."

"Oh, but I can't very well do that. I'm obliged to hand out one of these lovely gift baskets to every single passenger."

"We don't want one. Beat it."

"I'm afraid, sir, it's not as simple as that," persisted Gomez in his android voice. "My very position as social director of this train will be seriously jeopardized unless I personally distribute a basket of fruit and cheese to each and—"

"We hate fruit and loathe cheese. Get the hell away from here."

"Actually, sir, the railroad management doesn't really care if you eat the fruit and cheese or toss it down the dispozhole." Gomez drew out his stungun. "But you must sign this form indicating that you've received your basket. Until I get that squared away, I'm really afraid I cannot move along. And, you know, I still have to sign up people for the ElectroBingo tournament this afternoon after I distribute all these—"

"Shove the damn receipt under the door and I'll sign it. You can leave the basket out there."

"No. Oh, no. I simply couldn't do that. You see, the Second Class passengers aren't entitled to baskets this large. If one of them came along and spotted this one and took it, well, that would cause no end of trouble."

"Okay, okay. I'll open the damn door and you can hand me the damn paper to sign and the damn basket. Then you better clear out of here, buddy."

"Yes, fine. That will be just dandy." Gomez jumped, flattened himself against the wall next to the compartment doorway.

The door rattled, then slid open a few inches. "Okay," said the man from inside, "where the hell are you?"

Gomez remained silent, waiting.

"If you're so antsy about me signing your damn . . . Awk!"

A large shaggy man had thrust his head out into the corridor to look around for the social director and the basket of fruit and cheese.

The second Gomez saw him, he fired his stungun.

The beam hit the big man square in the left temple. It rendered him unconscious and he fell to his knees with a considerable thunk. Then he toppled forward, sprawling half into the corridor.

Gomez stayed where he was, gun ready.

A full minute passed, then another. No one else came out of the compartment.

Taking a deep breath, Gomez risked a look inside.

Slumped across the seat, hands bound behind her and a towel stuffed into her mouth, was the redhaired Natalie Dent.

Tucking away his gun, Gomez bent and dragged the big man back inside the room. "Fate is a funny thing, *cara*," he remarked to the Newz reporter. "It keeps throwing us together."

■

The dark green Customs robot blinked, made a faint whistling noise and pressed Jake's plas passport card to the scanner in its forehead once again. "Ah," it said.

"Something?" asked Jake.

"Ah," repeated the emerald robot as it rose up from behind its crimson desk.

"So you said." Jake was alone in this Customs cubicle. Beth and Agent MacQuarrie were being processed in other cubicles in a long string of tiny offices.

"You're Jake Cardigan." The robot tapped its index finger on the passport card.

"I am, yeah. Is there some problem?"

"If you'll wait here a moment, Mr. Cardigan." Leaving its red desk, the green robot walked out of the small Kyoto airport office. It took Jake's passport with it.

Jake, reminded of his interview with the assistant dean of Dan's school a few days ago, wondered if the Japanese authorities also thought he was a Tek dealer.

A slender Japanese in a white suit stepped into the office and coughed once. He was now holding Jake's passport card. "Pleased to meet you, Mr. Cardigan." Moving behind the robot's desk, he sat down.

"I don't know if I'm pleased to meet you or not," admitted Jake. "What's going on?"

"I'm Inspector Hachimitsu."

"Kyoto Police?"

The inspector nodded. "With the Murder Division."

Jake straightened up in his chair. "You're working on a case?"

"I am," answered Hachimitsu. "Do you know Norman Itoko?"

"Know his name. He's the operative with the Senuku Detective Agency who's going to . . . But he isn't going to be meeting me, is he?"

"No, Norman was killed a little over an hour ago."

"How?"

"Two assassins using lazguns killed him outside his home," said the inspector. "For good measure, they killed his wife as well when she came running out of the house."

"You knew him?"

"We were acquaintances. I was aware he was to contact you this morning."

"It's a Tek killing. Itoko must've found out something."

"If he did, he didn't confide in me." Inspector Hachimitsu held out Jake's passport. "I'd hate to see you killed as well, Mr. Cardigan. Especially in Kyoto. For your own protection, therefore, I'm seeing to it that you will be denied entry into our country and sent home to America at once."

⠶31⠶

omez had made a quick, thorough search of Natalie's train compartment before he untied her. "Tell me what happened, *chiquita*," he requested.

The angry reporter tugged the towel out of her mouth, spit lint and scowled up at him. "Don't think I'm not appreciative of your assistance, since I truly am," she said. "You might, however, in any future situations along this line, release me from bondage *first* and then do your snooping around my—"

"Nat, I wanted to make certain you weren't harboring any other louts." Kneeling beside the big man he'd stungunned, he started searching him. "As suspected, no trace of an ID packet. Any notion who this clunk is?"

"A safe assumption is that he's in the employ of one or more of the Tek cartels." She rubbed at her wrists. "He didn't, though, bother to introduce himself to me. He simply came barging in, slapped a hand over my mouth and started to truss me up. I managed to utter a faint cry for help, which I imagine you must have heard while lurking around outside and possibly contemplating some sort of electronic eavesdropping or—"

"I didn't even know you were aboard," he assured her as he extracted a lazgun from the unconscious hoodlum's shoulder holster. "For generations, however, the Gomez clan has been noted for rushing to the rescue of damsels in distress. Hearing a plea for succor, I automatically sprang into action."

"Oh, I see. I suppose, correct me if I'm wrong, that had you realized it was I who was being manhandled in here, you'd have continued on your way, whistling one of those inane ditties you're so fond of—"

"Nat, I recognized your distinctive tones in a matter of scant seconds." He located a stunrod in the thug's coat pocket, an electro-knife strapped to his calf. "But so ingrained is my impulse to help the helpless, that I popped into the fray, at great personal risk, to help you, even though you and I haven't always been the best of—"

"Popped right in? Good gravy, you dawdled out in that corridor nattering away in the offensive impersonation of a pansy for an inordinate length of time."

"Androids can't be pansies. It was only a couple of minutes." He stood, bent and caught hold of the lout by the armpits. "It was a pretty clever diversion, since it allowed me to deck this goon without any bloodshed whatsoever."

"I suppose, all things considered, you did do a fairly competent job of saving me from this bruiser."

Gomez opened the closet, worried the heavy unconscious man inside and managed to shove the door shut on him.

"You've dumped him right in on top of my suitcase," complained Natalie.

"He won't feel a thing, since he's out for at least twelve hours and by—"

"I really do hate to carp at every single thing, but I don't like the idea of that heavy hooligan crushing my dainty suitcase from here all the way to Tokyo, Gomez."

Sighing, muttering in Spanish, he reopened the closet, tugged out the small tan suitcase from beneath the slumbering thug, pushed him and prodded and got him shut in once again.

"I happen to speak Spanish very well, Gomez."

"*Muy bien.*" He dropped into the seat opposite her, smiling.

"I point that out now, since I would prefer that you don't continue to call me a streetwalker and a goat and other insulting names under your breath every time you get miffed over nothing at all."

His smile became more beatific. "Another thing that's genetically built into me is the ability to keep on being sweet and cordial to ladies even when they fail to pass along even so much as a small, pitiful thank you."

"I already thanked you."

"I missed it."

"If you'd do less whistling and talking to yourself, in my opinion, you might hear more of what's going on around you, especially in the area of gratitude." She brushed at her red hair. "Has anyone made an attempt on *you* since you boarded the train?"

"Not so far."

"Perhaps you were next on his list."

"We'll keep alert, in case he was traveling as part of a team," said Gomez. "Why would he want to do you any harm?"

"Somehow they've found out why I'm going to Tokyo."

"And why are you going to Tokyo, Nat?"

"Really now, you don't have to keep playing these silly games, the way you tried to do when our paths crossed enroute to The Casino." She gave a disappointed shake of her head. "Give me credit, since you know what a capable investigative reporter I am, for having found out about Dr. Hyaku on my own."

"Oh, yeah—Dr. Hyaku." Gomez had never heard the name before. "So you're working on that angle, too?"

"I already knew Hyaku was one of the top neobiologists in Japan as well as a former student of Dr. Chesterton," she said. "And I knew that Hyaku had disappeared a few months ago. But until I learned that Chesterton had vanished from the Freezer at almost the same time, I didn't see the significance."

"You know about Chesterton's being sprung, too?"

"Honestly, Gomez, do you think they give out top journalism prizes to nitwits?"

"Not usually, no," he said. "Are you suggesting, Nat, that we collaborate again—pool our resources in the hunt for the missing Hyaku?"

"We might as well, since that's the wisest course in the long run.

And we did function fairly smoothly together during our recent collaboration aboard The Casino," she said. "But, please, don't try to ditch me again the way you did the minute we got home to Greater Los Angeles. I actually had quite a few more questions I wanted to ask you."

"Dear lady," he lied, "I'll stick to your side throughout our stay in Tokyo."

■

Jake said, "We can do this two ways, Inspector—easy or hard."

"You're not in a position to threaten me, Mr. Cardigan."

"I am, though." Jake grinned. "That's, see, where you've miscalculated. Maybe because you didn't get enough information from Itoko."

"Are you saying that—"

"I'm saying the Cosmos Agency has a great deal of influence, which I'll use if I have to."

"Perhaps in Southern California it has some influence, but I assure you that—"

"We can sit around here and trade insults and flex our muscles," said Jake. "But it'll save a hell of a lot of time if you just call the head of the Senuku Detective Agency. He can fill you in on all the strings my agency pulled before I came over here, all the palms that were greased, all the—"

"Is this how you usually operate? By making shady deals behind the scenes?"

"If I have to, I do," he answered. "And Bascom, my boss, almost always works that way. He says it's a hell of a lot more efficient."

Hachimitsu dropped Jake's passport card on the red desk. "Norman Itoko didn't provide me with all the details on your proposed investigation in Kyoto," he said. "What were you intending to do?"

"I hope to find Dr. Gordon Chesterton."

"Hope is an odd word for a hardbitten detective to use."

"You've heard about the plague that's hit San Francisco. My former wife happens to be one of the victims," said Jake. "I suppose that gives me a personal reason along with all the professional ones."

"You believe Chesterton is in Kyoto?"

"A few months ago he was smuggled off the Freezer. It's possible he was shipped here, still in a suspended state. The proposed destination was the Arashi Warehouse Complex."

The inspector frowned. "We've long suspected, but have been unable to prove, a connection between Arashi and several major Asian Tek cartels."

"What about Tora Hokori?"

Hachimitsu didn't immediately answer. "The Tiger," he said finally. "She is supposed to have died."

"I don't think she did."

"Neither do I."

Jake asked him, "Could she be in Kyoto?"

"There have been rumors that she was headquartered in several cities including ours. As yet we have nothing tangible as to her true whereabouts," the Japanese said. "You suspect that Dr. Chesterton is working with her?"

"Sonny Hokori is probably the one who arranged to have Chesterton smuggled clear of the penal colony. That was so he could produce a new supply of his synthetic plague virus. After Sonny died, Tora must've carried on."

"You had a hand in his death, didn't you?"

"Not exactly, but I was there when it happened. Tora probably includes me on her list of those responsible."

The inspector said, "This manmade plague is being used for more than just terrorism."

Jake nodded. "They haven't issued any of their demands yet, but the Teklords are going to withhold the antidote unless all the countries of the world drop their campaigns against Tek," he said. "They'll use it on other cities, all across the globe, until they get what they want."

"They'll have to be stopped."

"I'm not the only one working on this, obviously," Jake told him. "But I want to try to find Chesterton and the antidote."

"Very well." Inspector Hachimitsu stood. "You can remain in Kyoto, but I'd like you to keep in close contact with me."

"Thanks, I will."

The policeman held out his hand. "It wasn't, let me mention, your threats that persuaded me. But rather the logic of your position."

"I thought I'd better try both," said Jake, shaking his hand. "One or the other usually works."

:: 32 ::

Jake slowed on his way to the vidphone alcove. "Who're you waving at?"

Beth turned away from the wide sliding glass doors of the living room. "Agent MacQuarrie's already taken up a position out there amidst the foliage."

"A dedicated fellow."

They were staying at an inn near the Kamo River and their living room faced on a large terraced garden. The early afternoon outside was blurred with mist.

"I've thought of an angle I'd like to work on," she told him.

"Sure, what is it?"

"If Chesterton was still in a state of suspended animation when he was brought here, then they'd need special equipment—and some uncommon drugs—to revive him."

"And if anybody hereabouts has ordered that sort of thing, then they're probably linked with Tora Hokori."

"It's a long shot, because they'd have been very cautious about how they gathered what they needed," Beth said. "I know somebody who's an associate prof at Kyoto Tech. He'll let me use their computer facilities."

"You seem to know guys on just about every spot on Earth."

"Basically I'm a very sociable person." She smiled. "This is an academic friend, Jake, not a former lover."

"Was I sounding jealous?"

The phone buzzed.

He hurried to the alcove. "Yeah?"

A small, thin Japanese woman of about thirty appeared on the screen, smiling shyly. "Mr. Jake Cardigan, please?"

"That's me."

"I'm Yoshiko Kiru," she said in a soft, gentle voice. "I was Norman Itoko's partner. Would it be possible for you and I to meet?"

"It would, yes. I was just going to call the detective agency."

"We might talk at the Golden Pavilion Teahouse in one hour. Is that possible for you?"

"Yes."

She told him how to find his way there and ended the call.

Jake punched out the number of the Senuku Agency.

A white enameled robot in a crimson kimono answered. "Senuku. How may I help you?"

"Do you have a Yoshiko Kiru working there?"

After three seconds the robot replied, "I have just consulted the employee roster, sir. The answer is no. May someone else help you?"

"No, thanks." He clicked off the screen.

Beth came over to stand behind him. "She's not really with the agency, huh?"

"Nope, she isn't."

"What are you going to do?"

Jake grinned. "Have tea with her."

■

The teahouse occupied a two-tiered gilded pagoda that sat in the center of a small clearing and was surrounded by tall pine trees. White gravel was laid out in swirling patterns on both sides of the wooden walkway leading to the front entrance.

As Jake, by himself, approached the Golden Pavilion someone inside suddenly bellowed in pain.

A teacup shattered, a chair fell over and then a large Japanese came stumbling rapidly backwards out into the afternoon. His head hit the wind chimes dangling next to the doorway and produced a quick disjointed tune. The big man half turned, went staggering by Jake, fell off the wood planking and dropped to his knees in the gravel.

Jake went on inside.

At a table near the entryway Yoshiko Kiru was dabbing at her jacket with a plyonapkin.

"I hope he didn't collide with you," she said.

"Nope. Who was he?"

"I have no idea, but he persisted in trying to join me."

"Management threw him out?"

"I threw him out. Won't you sit down, Mr. Cardigan?"

He sat down.

Nearby a robot waiter in a black kimono was gathering up the remains of a delicate teacup.

Jake said, "The Senuku Agency doesn't know that you were Itoko's partner."

"Yes, that's true. Our relationship was unofficial." The waiter placed a new cup in front of her. "I also shared an apartment with him."

Jake poured tea for her, then for himself. "He had a wife, too."

"He saw her infrequently. Unfortunately today was one of the times he chose to visit."

"If I mention you to Inspector Hachimitsu—will he know who you are?"

"Yes, I believe so." She sipped at her tea.

"Okay. You wanted to talk to me."

Yoshiko nodded. "Norman was looking forward to meeting you, to working with you," she told Jake. "In anticipation of your arrival, once he'd been briefed by your Cosmos Agency, he began making discreet inquiries. . . . Yes, I know. Obviously he wasn't discreet enough, since they must have realized what he was up to." She paused to take another sip of tea. "The crate you were interested in, the one that might possibly have contained the body of the gentleman you're interested in . . ." She smiled faintly. "I find I'm talking about Dr. Chesterton as though he were simply a piece of merchandise."

"To the Hokoris he was. Was Itoko able to find out anything about the crate?"

"Two things, yes," she replied. "That it was definitely delivered to the Arashi Warehouse Complex. Once there, however, all record of it was expunged."

Jake tapped the side of his cup with his forefinger. "That could mean Chesterton was in it and that they don't want anyone to trace him beyond here."

"Norman and I believe Kyoto was Chesterton's final destination."

"Why—is Tora here?"

"Norman suspected that she was. He planned, once you'd arrived, to help you find her."

He asked, "Can you help me do that?"

"I should like to try, Mr. Cardigan," she said quietly. "That is, if you trust me."

"I'm inclined to," he admitted. "But I'm going to have to do some checking first."

"I understand." She gave him her vidphone number. "Contact me once you're convinced I won't betray you."

"I'm sorry about Itoko."

"You never met him."

Jake said, "But I've met you."

::33::

She kept finding him.

No matter how deftly Gomez slipped out of his tiny, expensive room at the towering Kanashii Hotel and how careful he was to leave no trail, Natalie continually managed to track him down.

For instance, at a little after midday he was in the Star-Spangled Burgers restaurant on the edge of the Shinjuku neighborhood. Gomez had gone there to meet with the private investigators his detective agency had arranged for him to work with while he was in Tokyo.

"What a dump," commented Larry Kanzoo, returning to their small red table and holding out his tray to Gomez. "Does that look like a Double Gobchoker Burger to you?"

"Been a long time since I've viewed one, but it does seem close."

"Naw, they left off the flapping pickles." The Japanese private detective sat down.

"Maybe you ought to search more thoroughly through that pile of food for traces of—"

"And it's no use complaining. Naw, all the flapping robots behind the counter are designed to be surly. That's because this hole is based on an American burger joint. I hope to hell you feel at home here, Gomez."

"As a matter of fact, I'm more partial to Japanese fare. So if you lads would like to switch venue, it's fine with me."

"What a sewer this is," said Leroy Kanzoo, returning to the table. "Look what they're trying to pass off as a Double Fisherman's Dream Burger. The head's still on the flapping trout."

"It's supposed to be, Leroy," said his younger brother.

"Naw, it isn't. Check the pic on the vidmenu right in front of you."

"I did earlier and you can definitely see little beady fish eyes peering out at you from under the lettuce if you look very carefully. But quit complaining. Gomez says he loves this sinkhole, since it reminds him of home."

"On the contrary, gents," he said. "But let's turn to business."

"The shipping crate you're interested in." Leroy lifted the topmost bun and scowled at the fish lying there.

"We dug into the matter of that crate, which was delivered to the esteemed Chikatetsu Merchandise, Ltd., outfit," said Larry. "By the way, do we bill you direct for our services or send it along to Cosmos?"

"Cosmos. Now tell me about the—"

"I can't eat anything that looks back at me," complained Leroy.

"The crate," reminded Gomez, who wasn't eating anything.

Larry took a bite of his burger, chewed unenthusiastically for a moment. "You suspected that maybe some gink was stashed in the crate that was delivered to Chikatetsu on the date in question," he said finally.

"That's one possibility, sí."

"But not in this instance, Gomez," said Leroy. "This particular case was packed full to the brim with illegal Tek chips."

"You sure?"

The elder Kanzoo brother nodded. "The crate was seized by the Tokyo Drug Enforcement Bureau two days after it arrived."

Gomez frowned. "Nothing like that showed up on the records we checked."

"That's because the TDEB gink who did the seizing neglected to file a report."

Larry added, "Instead he made a substantial contribution to his retirement fund by peddling the Tek to certain shifty merchants around town."

"Then that means—"

"Oh, crap," said Leroy. "Here comes that carrot-topped bimbo again."

Glancing around, Gomez spotted Natalie Dent making her way through the tables toward him. "Join us for lunch, Nat?" he inquired cordially.

The redhaired reporter halted beside the table, stood surveying him with disappointment showing clearly on her face. "You haven't exactly stuck to our bargain."

"Goodbye, Gomez." Gathering up his burger, Larry departed.

"We'll keep in touch." Leroy followed his brother out, leaving his burger at the table.

Natalie sat down. "What have you found out about Dr. Hyaku?"

Gomez spread his hands wide. "Not a blessed thing, *carita.*"

"I come upon you consorting with a pair of the most unscrupulous private eyes in all of Tokyo, men whose reputations are so wretched that they make you look like a saint by comparison, and yet you claim none of you has come up with a blessed fact."

"I am a saint," he interrupted to assure her. "As soon as I find time to file all the proper forms, I'm sure to be canonized."

"Didn't those seedy Kanzoo brothers tell you anything of importance?"

"Nope, *nada.*"

Smiling with satisfaction, Natalie placed her small black purse on the table beside Leroy's abandoned plate. "My sources are, in this instance at any rate, considerably better than yours," she told him. "It appears that Dr. Nobu Hyaku, age forty-one and formerly a much respected neobiologist, has been for the past several months, if not longer, in the employ of the Hokori cartel and at present he's working directly with Tora Hokori."

"She's dead and done for," said Gomez guilelessly, "so I don't see how he could possibly be employed by—"

"Tora isn't dead at all, Gomez, although she really was seriously injured in a maglev train accident," said the reporter.

"Okay, *bonita,* I'll take your word for it. Tora is still extant and Doc Hyaku is working for her."

"What's more, Gomez—and, listen, I'm pretty near certain that you've been lying to me since we reached Tokyo, and I base that conclusion chiefly on the fact that nobody I know, most especially you, can bring off looking as innocent and pure as you're trying to look right this minute. Anyway, as I was about to say, Hyaku recruited, although corrupted might be the better word, at least two of his colleagues. Both of them experts in the same sort of biological weaponry area that the missing Dr. Chesterton excels in."

Gomez asked, "Do you know where Dr. Hyaku has gotten to?"

"All I've come up with so far is the possibility that he's with Tora in a temple she's using as her headquarters. The trouble is, in a city like Kyoto there are something like a thousand temples and shrines, so that zeroing in on the exact one is going to be difficult."

"Hold it, *almita.* Tora and the doc are allegedly in Kyoto now?"

"According to my sources, they are, yes." Opening her purse, she dipped a hand inside. "There is something else, and I'm the first to admit, even though you accuse me of fancying myself infallible, that I'm not quite certain what to make of it." She drew out a small, frayed photograph and handed it across to him. "An informant passed this on to me. It was taken, at considerable risk, in Kyoto a few weeks ago."

The picture showed a portion of a laboratory. On a white table in the foreground lay an incomplete female android. The head and torso were finished, however, and it was obviously a simulacrum of Tora Hokori. "This must have been taken in the workshop," speculated Gomez, "where they turn out their killer androids."

"Yes, but I can't exactly figure out why they would want to fashion a kamikaze dupe of Tora herself. Unless somehow they were—"

"Christ!" Gomez had noticed the nearly complete male android stretched out on the table directly behind the one that held the replica of Tora. "This is a sim of Agent MacQuarrie—one of the government guys assigned to look after Beth Kittridge."

"Then they must intend to kill her."

"Her or Jake—or both of them." He jumped to his feet. "I've got to make a call right now."

"You're not, please, going to attempt to ditch me once again, are you, Gomez?"

"I am not," he assured her. "Soon as I get back from the vidphone, I intend to accompany you to Kyoto with all haste."

Dodging tables and patrons, he sprinted to a phone alcove. He tried Jake's number at the inn in Kyoto, but got no answer. He settled for contacting the Senuku Detective Agency and telling an operative there to find Jake fast. And warn him.

⠹34⠹

gent MacQuarrie caught up with him a block from the teahouse. "Hey, Jake. Wait a minute." The government man came pushing through the tourists and pedestrians on the busy Kyoto sidewalk.

Stopping in front of a multistoried curio supermarket, Jake asked, "Why aren't you watching Beth?"

"One of my other men is. . . . But, Jake, listen. You'd better come along with me."

"Something wrong?"

MacQuarrie put a hand on Jake's shoulder. "We don't think she's in any danger of dying, but Beth is unconscious and—"

"What happened to her?"

The agent gave a sad shake of his head. "Hell, I don't know exactly," he admitted. "She came back to your rooms at the inn about a half hour ago and everything seemed fine. Then, a few minutes later, I heard a crash. I rushed inside to find her out cold on the floor of the bathroom."

"Is it the plague?"

"I don't think so, but we got a doctor in to look after her," said MacQuarrie. "I think maybe you ought to be with her, unless you're too busy with your—"

"No, I'm not too busy," he answered impatiently. "Is Beth still at the inn?"

"I told the doctor not to move her until we got back. You can ride over in my skycar."

"Sure, okay. Did she hurt herself in some kind of fall, do you think?"

"There's no evidence of that, Jake. I really haven't any idea of what exactly is wrong with Beth," said the agent. "I'm parked just around the corner."

Jake walked along beside him. "What does the doctor say—how serious is this?"

"Well, serious enough for me to come and fetch you."

■

Jake ran across the garden. The afternoon was chill and a thin mist still hung over the shrubs, miniature trees and colored gravel.

The sliding glass doors stood open; some of the mist had drifted into the living room.

There was no one in sight.

"Doctor—how is she?" called Jake, hurrying toward the bathroom.

For some reason the door was shut.

He yanked it open.

There was a body sprawled on the bright white floor.

But it wasn't Beth.

Lying on his back, his throat cut, was Inspector Hachimitsu.

"What the hell is going on?" Jake took one step back.

Then a sudden and overwhelming pain got hold of his body. It shook him and he struggled to fight it off. He stiffened, gasping for air. Then he fell over onto the bloody deadman.

Someone had used a stungun on him.

■

The fog was much worse.

The living room was thick with it.

The afternoon had grown much colder. Jake found he was shivering as he sat there on the futon. "Sorry, I didn't catch what you said," he mumbled apologetically.

Inspector Hachimitsu bowed politely in his direction. "I was asking how you were feeling, Mr. Cardigan."

Jake winced. "Wait now. Didn't I . . . didn't I find you in the john? You were dead."

"This is very unfortunate." The police inspector moved closer to him through the swirling mist. "I had been assured by your superiors that you were no longer addicted to Tek."

"I'm not a tekkie," insisted Jake. "I never used the stuff once I got out of the Freezer. Well, once on the first day out but never since then."

"Once, twice. Like most Tekheads, you've long since lost track of how many—"

"Your throat was cut. In there. Blood all over."

The Japanese tilted his head back, smiling sadly and tapped at his neck. "As you can see, Mr. Cardigan, I remain intact and alive."

Jake tried to get up, found he couldn't just yet. His legs hadn't returned entirely to his control. "Okay, let that pass for now. What I really want to know is how Beth is."

"I have no idea," replied Hachimitsu. "Do you feel well enough, after your recent bout with Tek, to—"

"Hey, I don't know exactly what's going on, Inspector. But I am damn sure I haven't been using any—"

"Oh, so? Then all the paraphernalia beside you on the table belongs to someone else, does it, Mr. Cardigan?"

Jake hadn't noticed the low black table before, nor what was atop it. This was Tek gear sure enough. The small black Brainbox, the electrodes to attach to your skull, a scatter of five cockroach-size Tek chips. "Somebody's trying to frame me."

"Again?"

"There's no rule says you can only be framed once."

"Please, allow me to ask you what I came to ask you, Mr. Cardigan. Are you up to identifying someone for me?"

"I suppose so, I don't know. Can't you tell me where Beth is?"

"Have you looked in the bathroom?"

"I already did that. Can you maybe shut the doors and keep some of this damn fog out of here?"

"The people I want you to identify are waiting out there in the garden. Are you certain you looked in the bathroom, Mr. Cardigan?"

"Sure, I am. That's where I found you. With your throat cut."

The inspector smiled sympathetically. "Do you know this person?"

From the fog outside stepped Kate. She was gaunt, hollowcheeked and wearing a wrinkled, bloodstained hospital gown. "This is really so typical of you, Jake. Dragging me out of bed to come over here and help you on this case of yours."

"Kate, I had nothing to do with—"

"Do you know this woman?" the inspector asked him.

"She's my wife. No, wait. Used to be. She used to be my wife."

"I'm dying, Jake. The least you can do is admit we're married."

"But we're not. You divorced me while I was up in the Freezer."

"Who told you that? Was it that little whore you're sleeping with?"

"Do you know this person?"

Dan came in from out of the fog. He was wearing a dirty hospital gown, too.

"Dad, you promised me you were going to help us. But you've just kept screwing things up and now Mom and I are going to die."

"You're not dead, Dan. You're still up and around."

"These people are both closely connected with the spreading of the plague in San Francisco," charged Inspector Hachimitsu. "I intend to hold them for—"

"Don't let him, Jake." Kate was beside him now. "He'll hurt Danny."

"My son doesn't have a damn thing to do with—"

"We'll let the courts decide that, Mr. Cardigan."

"Stop him, Jake." Kate placed a knife in his hand.

Jake frowned down at the weapon. There was already blood smeared on the long, sharp blade. "Inspector, I won't let you arrest my son."

"Kill him, Jake!"

Jake made a desperate effort and was able to stand up. He started, stumbling some, toward the policeman.

"Go ahead," Kate urged again, "kill him."

⠿35⠿

Jake lunged at the inspector, trying to slash him with the knife. Hachimitsu easily dodged him. Smiling, bowing mockingly, he retreated into the thick fog that had filled the living room.

Jake lost sight of him. Then he spotted a figure in the drifting mist. But it didn't seem to be the policeman.

All at once the fog was gone. Jake was sitting on the floor, the bloody knife held loosely in his right hand.

"How're you doing, *amigo?*"

"You're not Hachimitsu."

"A good thing, too. If I was, I'd be dead on the floor of your bathroom. How do you feel?"

"Sid?" Jake shook his head, slowly, from side to side. "I'm not quite sure . . . what the hell is going on?" He noticed he was hooked up to the Tek Brainbox that was supposed to be sitting on the black table.

Except there wasn't any table.

"I know it's risky to stop a Tek session before the chip runs out," said his partner, who was squatting next to him. "But I decided to risk using the turnoff button on the gadget you're connected to."

"Feels like I'm coming out of it okay. I don't think I'm likely to have any negative side effects."

"What would you say to standing up?"

Jake considered that while he, gingerly, detached the electrodes and discarded the Tek gear on the floor. "I think I can stay on my feet, once up." With Gomez helping him, he got shakily to an upright position. "How come you're not in Tokyo?"

"I journeyed here fast as I could to let you know that MacQuarrie might be an andy."

"He might be, yeah. Not a kamikaze, though."

"No, they apparently decided to get rid of you in a nastier way. By killing an important local cop and making it look as though you'd knifed him while in a Tek stupor."

"Tekkies rarely kill people while using the stuff."

"We know that, but it might be tough to convince the Kyoto constabulary of that right off. Especially if they'd popped in here and found the inspector dead in the john and you sprawled there with a bloody knife in one hand and a Brainbox in the other."

"MacQuarrie—the android MacQuarrie I guess that would be— he told me Beth had been hurt," he said, remembering. "He brought me back here to the inn. I saw Inspector Hachimitsu's body and then . . . Yeah, MacQuarrie used a stungun on me. Thing must've been at the lowest setting, so I was only out for a few minutes. While I was unconscious, he hooked me up to this damn Tek gear." Jake let it drop to the floor, along with the blood-smeared knife. "He set the Brainbox to spin out an hallucination for me about killing the inspector."

"Not a bad scheme, and one that takes advantage of your past record. They get rid of an annoying local policeman and also incapacitate you for a while," said Gomez. "I'd guess the cops are being alerted about now—or they could be already wending their way here."

"I've got to find Beth—I'm worried about her."

"Any notion where to find her?" Gomez knelt near the knife, fished a small metal rod out of his side pocket.

Jake glanced up at a floating ball-clock. "She's due to visit a professor friend of hers about now. We're supposed to meet near there in a half hour."

"I suggest you borrow my aircar and hasten there." Clicking on the rod, which caused it to glow an intense orange, he passed it along the knife. "This'll erase all traces of your having handled what I imagine must be the murder weapon."

"Can you face the local law by yourself?" Jake moved, still shaky on his legs, to the open doorway.

"Keep in mind that I've been married three times—or is it four by now?—in this life thus far," reminded Gomez. "I can explain my way out of most anything."

"Where do you want to meet later?"

"I happen to be sharing a discreet hideaway with a friend of mine from the media." He gave him an address. "The alley door is the one to use, *amigo.*"

"Would your newsperson chum be Natalie Dent?"

"That's who, *si.* Can't seem to elude that titian-haired lass."

"I'm expecting some information from an informant—you know him, it's Timecheck. I'll tell him to contact me there, if that's—"

"That's fine. But you'd best depart *muy pronto.*"

From far off had come the sound of approaching police skyvans.

■

The courtyard of Professor Anthony Nikuya's home was blurred with chill, grey fog. Jake made his way cautiously along the white gravel path toward the low, sprawling house.

Suddenly up ahead on his right a stand of artificial bamboo rattled.

Jake whipped his stungun free of its holster.

He could make out something in the fog. A dark, crouching shape.

Gun in hand, he approached it.

On hands and knees in front of the high, thin rods of yellow bamboo was a chromeplated robot wearing a black neosilk kimono. The top of its skull was no longer there, the inner workings dangled out, smoldering.

Giving one final convulsive rattle, it collapsed at Jake's feet.

He crouched slightly, moving slowly closer to Professor Nikuya's house.

The sliding plastiglass doors were gone. They had been shot away and shards of glass were scattered across the foyer.

Jake found a second robot there. This one was lying on its back, a large jagged hole burned in its metal chest.

In the hallway beyond a tea set had fallen and smashed. A delicate white teapot, with cherry blossoms painted on its side, was in three pieces near the doorway of one of the rooms. The tea had spilled out of it like blood out of a wounded animal.

Holding his breath for a few seconds, Jake stood listening.

Then he entered the room.

It was an office and a small, slim Japanese of about forty sat behind the desk.

There was no one else in the study with him.

The man, who was probably Nikuya, was alive. But a powerful stungun had been used on him and Jake estimated he'd be out for another dozen hours at least.

He noticed that the computer terminal built into the desk had been activated. Using a few tricks he'd picked up over the years, Jake persuaded the terminal to talk to him.

"How may I serve you, sir?" it inquired in an extremely polite voice.

"Was Professor Nikuya consulting you just now?"

"Yes, that is so."

"Was there anyone else here with him?"

"A young woman, judging from the sound of her voice. Woman, not android. He addressed her as Beth."

"What happened?"

"Two other voices intruded, male. The woman cried out. A sound that must have been that of a stunrifle came next. Then a brief struggle, followed by a stungun. After that, silence. Is the Professor alive?"

"He is, yeah. What was he asking you about?"

"He, and the young woman, were apparently interested in the activities over the past few months of the Yakuhin Pharmaceutical Company of Kyoto. He had only just begun to inquire about the company, however, when the intruders—"

"Put your gun aside, Mr. Cardigan," ordered a voice from the doorway. "Then, if you'd be so kind, raise your hands."

⠸36⠸

The man with the lazgun in his left hand was Japanese. He was plump, wore a pale-green suit and had a wide, dimpled smile. "Stand clear of the desk, Mr. Cardigan." Stepping around the shattered tea things in the hallway, he came into the room. He smelled strongly of sandalwood.

Jake followed instructions. "That's an impressive perfume you're wearing," he observed. "Who are you?"

"My favorite scent and, perhaps, I tend to overdo it," admitted the plump Japanese, his smile growing wider. "Let us simply say that I'm affiliated with the Hokori cartel."

"You stayed behind after they grabbed Beth, huh?"

"Yes, in the event that you were able to evade the trap set for you and came here seeking your paramour. A wise move, as it turns out."

"So you guys have Beth?"

"She's in our hands."

"Why?"

"It was felt she'd make a useful hostage," he replied. "And there is apparently some interest in consulting her on technical matters."

"About the plague?"

The smile stretched even wider. "I suggest you come along with me now."

"To see Tora Hokori?"

"It will be best if you simply accompany me, reserving any further questions for later." He gestured toward the doorway with his lazgun. "My aircar is parked in the lane behind the house."

Shrugging one shoulder, Jake started for the exit.

The smiling Japanese moved in close behind him.

Two steps beyond the threshold Jake said, "Damn." He seemed to slip on the spilled tea and his right foot went sliding.

He twisted, made a grab for the Japanese to keep himself from falling.

That only succeeded in sending them both crashing to the floor.

Jake then chopped the gun out of the other man's grasp, got himself quickly upright and then planted a forceful kick square in his groin.

While the Japanese doubled in pain, Jake stepped over him and scooped up the fallen lazgun. He then darted into the den to retrieve his abandoned stungun.

Back in the hall he said to the fallen gunman, "Now you're going to tell me where they have Beth."

Wincing, the Japanese made it to his feet. "Your conduct has been most ungentlemanly," he said disapprovingly.

"Yeah, it has," admitted Jake, grinning. "Where is she?"

"You and I operate under entirely different codes of ethics." He all at once brought his right hand up to his mouth. "I have no intention of betraying the . . ."

The poison he'd gulped down was quick and efficient. He fell to the floor and was dead in under ten seconds.

Jake frowned down at him. "Damn," he said again.

■

"Wrestlers yet again," observed Gomez, scowling, thrusting his hands deep into his trouser pockets and coming in sideways out of the misty afternoon alley.

"At least they're not hussies, like that batch you insisted on liberating from The Casino," said Natalie as she shut the office door after him. "We were, I might mention, extremely lucky to get this abandoned facility for our use as a temporary base and if it weren't for the fact that I have several highly helpful colleagues here in . . . Oh, Gomez, what happened to your face?"

He crossed over to the desk, which was piled high with gloposters announcing long-ago events held here at the RoboSumo Palace. "I was detained by a somewhat protracted discussion with several of Kyoto's finest."

"But you're bruised and battered." She stood watching him, hands clasped together in front of her.

"In its initial stages our chat was a trifle boisterous," he admitted, sitting down, gingerly, in the wobbly desk chair. "That's what happens when the cops walk in and find you with the corpse of one of their own inspectors."

"Which inspector was that?"

Gomez, his deep frown never deserting him, recounted for her what had gone on at Jake and Beth's rooms at the inn.

"But finally the police must have listened to reason," Natalie said after he concluded. "I mean, you're here."

"They mostly listened to threats, coming from Bascom's Japanside connections."

"What about Beth Kittridge—where is she?"

"Jake went hunting for her. Hasn't he showed up here yet?"

Natalie shook her head. "No, he hasn't," she replied. "However, a really dreadful man showed up here a few moments ago claiming to be an informant of Jake's."

"Yeah, Jake was going to tell the guy to meet him here."

"Well, he showed up."

Gomez got to his feet. "So where is he?"

"Over there." The redhaired reporter pointed.

"I don't see him."

"On the floor with the robot wrestlers."

Stacked against the far wall were six fat robot sumo wrestlers in full costume. Sprawled in front of the two neat piles was a thin young Chinese in a long plaid overcoat.

"Hey, that's Timecheck. What did you do to the guy?"

"Well, he seemed very furtive and seedy-looking to me, so when he persisted in—"

"Of course the lad is furtive, *chiquita*. That's one of the characteristics of his trade."

"I only used my stungun on its lowest setting, so he ought to be coming around any second now."

Timecheck stirred and groaned. "Woops," murmured the Chinese as he sat up and shook his head. "What time is it?" He rolled up the right sleeve of his rumpled overcoat, revealing a silverplated metal arm studded with over a dozen watch faces.

"That's another thing that annoyed me about him," Natalie whispered to Gomez. "He kept offering to tell me what time it was in various dull cities around the—"

"Exactly 4:16 here in Kyoto," said the thin young man as Gomez helped him up. "Hiya, Sid, good to see you again. We had some great times together when I was living in Greater LA, huh? Jake here yet?"

"He'll arrive shortly."

"If we were in Ethiopia now, it would be exactly—"

"Timecheck, do you have something important to pass along to Jake?"

The informant was looking sourly in Natalie's direction. "This quiff a pal of yours?"

"Business associate merely."

"Jeez, you're not balling her, are you?" asked Timecheck.

"No, no, nay." Gomez led him over, settled him in the desk chair. "Sit down, collect your scattered wits."

"I'd really like to believe," continued Natalie, "that if you were forced to choose between me and a shabby tipster from the lower depths that you wouldn't hesitate to—"

"*Bastante*, enough," Gomez warned her with a pleasant smile.

"I got only the fondest memories of providing information for you and Jake," said Timecheck, bringing one of the watches up close to his eyes. "Huh . . . Poughkeepsie time is running about eighteen secs slow. Must be an aftereffect of getting zozzled by this skirt's stunner.

Going to have to add repair costs to your tab, Sid, unless I can patch it myself. Let me tell you, friend to friend, you maybe ought not to hang out with any dame who is so quick to shoot down innocent bystanders or—"

Someone had tapped on the door.

Checking a security monitor, Natalie announced, "Good, it's Jake."

"About time," commented Timecheck.

::37::

She awoke in darkness.

Beth found herself lying on her back, staring up into thick blackness. Wherever she was, it was cold and damp.

Her body hurt. She was overly aware of just about every bone that made up her skeleton and all of them ached. Her skin itched, burned. She could hear her pulse beating loudly in her ears.

When Beth blinked, enormous glaring yellow flowers blossomed all around her in the black. Pressing her hands down beside her, she felt some sort of smooth, soft fabric.

They'd used a stungun on her, the memory of that came back to her now. Two men, large and dressed in black, had come bursting into the study. The one with the silvery stunrifle had shot Tony Nikuya. The other man, whose eyeballs seemed to protrude through the slits in his tight silken hood, had used his stungun on her as she'd tried to get around behind the desk to help Tony.

She concentrated on breathing, slowly and carefully in and out, for a moment. Sharp pains zigzagged across her chest each time she inhaled.

"I wonder," she said to herself, "if those fellows are some of Tora Hokori's people."

They probably were, which meant Beth was somewhere in Tora's headquarters.

She moved her right hand further out from her body. Presently she felt just chill air instead of cloth. Closing her fingers, she got hold of the edge of what felt like a floating cot.

Beth pulled hard, got herself to a sitting position with her feet touching the stone floor. The motion caused more yellow flowers to explode in the darkness. This time jagged crimson bars of light flashed between the bursts of yellow.

Gradually the flashes subsided, along with the nausea she'd felt as soon as she sat up.

"They didn't kill me on the spot—why?"

Maybe because they had something else in mind.

Somewhat reluctantly Beth let go of the cot and attempted to stand up.

That made her dizzy again, made her see splashes of light where there really wasn't any light. The aftermath of being stungunned was rougher than she'd heard.

Very slowly, sliding one foot at a time across the stone floor, Beth started walking.

"It could be that Tora just wants to use me as a hostage."

But maybe things weren't that simple. Maybe it was part of some plan to trap Jake, to kill him.

"Easy now," she warned herself. "You don't have enough information."

She walked ten slow, careful paces through the darkness. Halting, she reached out in front of her with one hand. Her fingers encountered nothing. She turned completely around, hand held out, and still touched nothing.

Beth resumed her patient, sliding walk.

She wondered, "How long have I been unconscious?"

No way of telling really. Depending on the setting, a stungun blast could knock you out for anywhere from a few minutes to fifteen hours or more.

Beth covered another ten steps, then stopped and felt out all around her once more. Still no sign of a wall.

She began to walk again.

Then, silently and unexpectedly, a huge glaring rectangle of bright white light appeared directly in front of her.

∎

Timecheck tapped one of his watches, squinting at it. "Berkeley time isn't working at all," he complained.

Jake was sitting on the edge of the desk, one leg slowly swinging back and forth. "Better get right to the information you have for me," he advised slowly and evenly.

"Yes, sure, sorry." He pulled down his coat sleeve, dropped both arms to his sides. "You asked me to check on various transportation possibilities occurring in the vicinity of a certain warehouse on specific days a few months ago."

"What did you get?"

Timecheck started to consult another of his watches, then suddenly thought better of it. "I'm pretty sure I've come up with what you want, Jake. At approximately 10:17 A.M. on the second day in question an old bundled-up geezer in a robochair was picked up behind the warehouse and loaded into a vehicle from the Rakuda Skycab Company."

"Yeah, that sounds like what we want," Jake said. "Where was the passenger taken?"

"To the Kenkoo Spa, that's in the foothills near Mount Hei."

Natalie, sitting in a folding chair near the stacked sumo wrestlers, exclaimed, "Bingo." Then, looking from Gomez to Jake, added, "Excuse me."

Jake asked the slim informant, "Anything else?"

"I ran a check on Yoshiko Kiru for you."

"Yeah?"

"Clean. She really was Itoko's quiff—and she helped the poor bozo with his private eye work."

"Thanks." Jake handed him some Banx notes.

"Anytime you hit town, call on me." Without counting it, Timecheck slipped the money into a lumpy overcoat pocket and took his leave.

As soon as the door shut, Jake turned to the redhaired Natalie. "What was the outburst about?"

"While I was cooling my heels here," she replied, "I got in touch with a few local contacts of my own. I'm pretty certain that Dr. Hyaku is using part of that same Kenkoo Spa as a secret lab."

"Who is he?" asked Jake.

"An illustrious neobiologist who disappeared at about the same time Chesterton was taking his leave of the Freezer," supplied Gomez. "He appears to be gainfully employed by dear little Tora these days."

"The man is obviously working on the manufacture of the synthetic plague virus the Teklords are using," said Natalie. "And I take it you believe the old gentleman in the wheelchair was Dr. Chesterton."

"Yep, I asked Timecheck to find out about any unusual passengers who were picked up in the vicinity of the warehouse about the time the crate was delivered there."

"What crate? Gomez, have you been holding back on—"

"Only one small tile, *cara*, in the overall mosaic of his caper," he assured her. "Don't fret, *por favor*."

"You're a very difficult man to put any long-term faith in."

Gomez turned toward Jake. "You haven't said anything about Beth yet, *amigo*. But she didn't come here with you and you're not looking especially cheerful."

"They've got her." He told them what had taken place at the professor's home.

"Stunguns used twice," said Gomez. "That indicates they didn't kill her either." He nodded at Natalie. "You still carrying around that photo?"

"Yes, here." She produced it from her purse, handed it to him and he passed it over to Jake.

"That's how I got wise to the existence of the Agent MacQuarrie sim," said his partner. "But note the more obvious fact to be gleaned from this illuminating example of the photographer's art. Namely that they were, in fairly recent times, also constructing a Tora android."

Jake studied the picture. "Maybe because that maglev train wreck did her serious damage afterall."

"Beth is an expert on androids, isn't she?"

"Sure, she helped construct the replica that I . . . that I worked with down in Mexico." He set the picture down atop one of the stacks of old wrestling posters. "Could be Tora wants to consult her."

"And could be they won't kill her right off because of that."

"The next thing to do," suggested Natalie, "is get a look inside the spa."

"I'd like to see the floor plans of the place." Jake walked over to the vidphone alcove. "And probably Yoshiko Kiru can help us with that."

⠶38⠶

They were robots, a pair of them, large and broad. They had black enameled bodies that glistened in the harsh white light out in the corridor.

One of them, saying nothing, came lumbering into the room. It made a beckoning gesture toward Beth.

"Where to?" she asked. Her voice sounded a little rusty to her.

The big robot simply repeated the come-along gesture.

Nodding, she moved to the opening in the wall.

The other robot, noting that Beth was a little unsteady on her feet, took hold of her left arm just above the elbow.

"Ouch, hey," she said. "Too tight."

The gleaming black mechanism paid no attention to her complaint. It started along the winding stone corridor, keeping a tight hold on her.

The other robot fell in beside them.

Turning to him, Beth asked, "Could you suggest to your partner that he loosen his grip?"

The mechanical man continued to look straight ahead, making no response.

Beth decided that protesting wasn't going to help. She tried to think of other things besides the painful grasp of the strong metallic fingers on her arm.

Rods of light ran along the low stone ceiling, giving off a harsh,

whitish glare. It was the sort of light that made you want to shield
your eyes.

The robots escorted her through what felt to be at least two miles
of twisting tunnel. Beth had the impression that the cell she awoke
in must have been deep underground and that they had been climbing upward.

They came to a high, wide teakwood door. Both robots halted.
Nearly a half minute passed before the door, creaking, swung open.

The black robot let go of her, the other one gave her a forward
shove. Beth went stumbling ahead as the big teak door shut behind
her.

She was in a vast, chill circular room. The ceiling was so high
above her that it was lost in shadows. About a hundred yards in front
of her rose an immense golden Buddha, seated on a jade pedestal.
It was at least a full hundred feet high and glowed a pale amber in
the dim, watery light of the enormous room.

Rubbing at her arm, she took a few tentative steps in the direction
of the Buddha. Each of her unsteady, shuffling steps echoed in the
huge, cold room.

"Good afternoon, Miss Kittridge."

There was a highback wicker chair in the deep shadows at the base
of the towering gilded Buddha. Slumped in the chair was the figure
of a darkhaired young woman, wearing dark trousers and a dark shirt.

"You must be Tora Hokori." Beth approached the seated figure.

"Not exactly."

Closer now, Beth noticed that the young woman in the chair had
blank staring eyes and that she wasn't breathing. Stopping a few feet
from the chair, Beth said, "This is only an android duplicate."

"Come over here, please."

Beth realized that the voice hadn't been coming from the
slumped android.

In the shadows behind the highback chair sat an array of complex,
bulky medical equipment, plus terminals, monitoring units and a
voxbox. Resting on a small white table, with an intricacy of twisting
colored wires spiderwebbing out from it, was a large chromed cylinder.

"The train accident," said Beth softly.

"My body," explained Tora Hokori's voice from the voxbox, "didn't survive the wreck."

"But they saved your brain."

"Yes, we have extremely skilled people working for us. We can afford them obviously—and we have other ways of acquiring them."

Beth glanced over at the silent android. "Not quite skilled enough apparently."

"Thus far, no," admitted Tora. "For some reason my new body continues to reject my brain."

Beth said, "Pity."

"That's one of the things I wish to talk to you about," the voxbox informed her. "Providing, that is, you're interested in remaining alive."

■

"Golly, what a story." In her enthusiasm Natalie nearly backed into three of the stacked sumobots. "This'll give me a terrific angle and, despite the critics who share your view, Gomez, that I'm a cold, heartless reporter, it will demonstrate that I'm capable of finding my way through to the human angle in what is otherwise a grim yarn of—"

"Button your *boca*," advised Gomez, cordially taking hold of her arm.

"But even you ought to be able to see this'll make a great lead," persisted the redhead. "Hardbitten, grizzled private op pauses in his pursuit of vicious Teklords to phone Frisco and determine the fate of his own plague-stricken family and—"

"*Bastante*," Gomez said to her as Jake stepped clear of the vidphone alcove. "What's the latest news on Kate, *amigo?*"

"Everything's about the same as it was when I left California," he answered.

"That's good, isn't it?"

"Dan doesn't think so." Jake sat, somewhat wearily, at the desk, moving aside two of the stacks of old posters. "I still have the feeling he believes I'm letting him down."

"That's a standard impression all kids his age try to give," said his partner. "I worked the same dodge on my *padre* back then."

"What a great angle," murmured Natalie. "Jake, would you mind telling me if you—"

"No more inquiries, *chiquita.*"

Jake spread out the maps and charts that Yoshiko Kiru had just vidfaxed to him. "Here's the Kenkoo Spa and environs."

Pulling free of Gomez's grip, Natalie moved forward and jabbed a finger at the topmost map. "Bingo," she said.

Jake looked up at her. "Now what?"

"Well, just take a gander at what lies less than half a mile from the darn spa." Her finger tapped a spot on the map. "That happens to be the Juunigwatsu Temple. It's one, I learned after some diligent digging, that's been shut down and untenanted for several years. We already know, at least I'm convinced of the fact, that Tora Hokori has a hidden headquarters in a temple right here in Kyoto. So there's an abandoned temple and it's within sneaking distance of the spa where Dr. Hyaku is almost certainly holed up churning out the plague virus."

"Yeah," acknowledged Jake, "it could be the same temple she's using as a base."

Gomez studied the map over his partner's shoulder. "Be that as it may, we have to concentrate on getting into the Kenkoo Spa first."

"But while you two fellows are doing that," said the redhead, "I can explore the situation at the temple."

Gomez shook his head. "No, that's far from smart. Bearding the lion—or in this case the tiger—in her lair isn't the thing to do right now."

"Darn it, Gomez, you persist in assuming that I'm utterly incompetent."

"It would be best," Jake told her, "if you wait until we've investigated the spa."

"But—"

"A firstclass reporter," suggested Gomez, "is also a good listener."

"I can listen and talk at the same time. And I really think that—"

"Take a look at this set of plans." Jake turned to another sheet. "There seems to be an entire floor beneath the main building of the spa."

"Be a nifty place," observed Gomez, "to stick a clandestine lab."

"You get down there by way of this passway near the public baths area."

Gomez backed up. "Any idea on how we get ourselves inside the spa initially?"

Jake grinned. "A few."

⠿39⠿

"Next time we flip a coin," grumbled Gomez.

"Your shawl is slipping," said Jake.

It was dusk and they were moving across the landing area next to the Kenkoo Spa. The oncoming night was cold, the mist was growing thicker again. The blossoms on the dozens of cherry trees that surrounded the spa were grey and sooty.

Gomez, his shoulders hunched and covered with a bright scarlet shawl, was riding along in a gunmetal robochair. "I still don't know why I volunteered for this part."

"Because you make a more convincing invalid than I do." Jake was wearing a white medical jacket.

"On the contrary, *amigo,* I happen to be bursting with vigor." His chair carried him down the gravel path toward the spa.

The building was large and had a crimson and gold pagoda-style roof. Sooty doves were roosting on it, cooing.

"In a way, even though she's been some help," said Jake, walking beside the chair, "I wish you hadn't invited Natalie Dent."

"I had little or no choice in the matter. She's a very determined *muchacha,*" said his partner. "First place, she rightly senses that much of what I do is extremely newsworthy. Secondly . . . well, hell, I don't like to sound vain, but I really think the lass has a crush on me."

"Isn't it odd how tough it is sometimes to tell the difference between love and loathing?" observed Jake. "At least for an outsider like me."

"Her pretended dislike is all part of the game," explained Gomez as they reached the wide plastiglass doors. "It's a shame I'm so dutifully married just now. Not that I'd want to get entangled with Nat, but all sorts of other women do continue to hurl themselves at me." As the doors hissed open, Gomez slumped further in his rolling chair and gave out a few feeble groans.

The Reception Room was large and had a miniature waterfall and a rock garden at its center. Seated at a wide Lucite desk near the splashing fountain was a handsome blond android wearing a full-length offwhite kimono. "Ah, you must be Mr. Chavez." Rising up and chuckling, he came toward them. "Dr. Ahiru phoned to make an appointment for you, sir."

"Ah, the power of bribery," said Gomez under his breath.

"Sir, I'm sure just one half-hour session in one of our marvelous Taiyoo Suites and you'll notice a very positive change. You must be Mr. Chavez's male nurse," he said, turning to Cardigan.

"That I am," agreed Jake.

"I don't know if either of you gentlemen is familiar with the Japanese language, but *taiyoo* means sun," the android explained. "In his suite Mr. Chavez will be treated with our special simulated sunray that is guaranteed to—"

"Doc Ahiru already gave me the spiel," cut in Gomez. "Let's simply get to the damn suite, huh?"

"Cranky and impatient." Chuckling, the android turned to Jake and winked. "Lots of them are when they first come to us here." He clapped his hands.

A chromeplated robot in a short crimson kimono entered the room, bowing first to the android and then to the seated Gomez. "How may I assist you, sir?"

"Juuku, escort Mr. Chavez and his nurse to Taiyoo Suite #16, please."

"It shall be done." Bowing again, Juuku turned and walked toward a nearby arched doorway.

Gomez and his chair went rolling after him.

"I sure hope this does him some good," Jake confided in the android before following the other two.

They moved down a long empty corridor whose walls were filled with animated murals based on the paintings of Hokusai.

At the doorway to Suite #16 the silvery robot stopped, bowing again.

Gomez smiled, slipped a stungun out from under his bright shawl and shot the robot.

Jake caught the mechanical man and, after his partner had jumped clear of the chair, dumped him into it.

The door of #16 whirred open, the chair and the disabled robot went rolling in and the door shut.

Gomez bowed to Jake. "Let's descend," he invited.

■

Wearing a long skyblue kimono that masked his clothes and carrying a plyosponge and a plaspak of cleansing solution, Gomez came sauntering amiably along the deadwhite corridor. "Evening, gents. Which way to the pool?"

Both the thickset Japanese guards popped to their feet out of their white wicker chairs. Each drew a lazgun from a hip holster, each pointed his weapon at the intruder. Just behind them was a narrow metal door.

"You made a mistake, buddy," the larger of the two informed him, making a go-away motion with his gun. "The baths are out in the other direction."

Gomez smiled apologetically, glancing up at the deadwhite ceiling and then around at the deadwhite walls. He spotted no sign of a spy camera. "How about that?" he said, shaking his head. "My wife told me I—well, she's not exactly my wife, you know, although we are traveling as mister and missus. That's because you get a much better rate that way in most of—"

"Take a hike," suggested the other guard. He returned his gun to its holster and sat again in his white chair. "This part of the spa is closed to the public."

"Is it now? Fancy that." Gomez chuckled. "I was just telling my wife—well, you know who I mean. I was telling her that half the temples in this damn town seem to be closed to the public. But I figure, because of my serious heart condition—it's one of these new plas ones and they can't seem to keep the damn motor working right. I figure I should be admitted just about anywhere, since my time is probably limited and if I don't see this stuff now, why—"

"Your time is really going to be limited, buddy, unless you haul your butt out of here." Putting a hand on Gomez's shoulder, the larger guard started pushing him along the corridor.

Around a bend they came to the teakwood door Gomez had used to come in. "You lads can't see this portal from where you sit," he remarked.

"We're more interested in the door we sit in front of."

"Isn't that inter . . . oh, mother of mercy! The motor's conking." Gomez gasped, staggered, dropped to the corridor floor. He stretched out his back, legs kicking.

"Hey, you can't go having a fit here." Holstering his gun, the big man knelt.

The teakwood door swung open suddenly. Jake, stungun in hand, stepped through and fired at the guard.

"Bingo, as they say." Gomez quietly got up. "There aren't any security cams in the corridor, *amigo*. Shall we work a similar dodge on the remaining guard?"

■

"*Seis.* That makes an even half-dozen louts downed thus far," remarked Gomez, catching the bulky guard he'd just stungunned. He arranged him neatly in a sitting position against the blank deadwhite wall of the underground corridor.

"Seven," corrected Jake.

"Oh, *sí.* I neglected to include the one you felled two bends back."

Jake said, "According to Yoshiko's floor plan, this main corridor is going to split up ahead."

"I'll take the lefthand road," offered his partner. "If we can't rally back at the fork in, say, fifteen minutes, then we'll come hunting for each other."

"Agreed," said Jake.

::40::

r. Chesterton was a tall, lanky man. His sparse head of hair was a dusty straw color, his white lab smock was wrinkled and stained. There was nothing but a low black couch in the big whitewalled office. "I usually take a nap about this time each evening," he said, sitting up, brushing at his hair with the knobby fingers of his left hand.

Jake stopped just inside the doorway, watching the man. He said nothing.

"You're Cardigan, aren't you?"

Jake nodded.

"I thought so. She showed me pictures of you. She has quite a collection. Side views, front views, long shots, closeups." He brushed at his hair with the knobby fingers of his right hand. "She didn't literally show them to me, didn't actually hand them to me. That's not possible right now. Had them shown to me. Tora doesn't much like you. Considers you an obstacle. May I ask you something?"

"Sure." Jake walked a few steps closer to the scientist.

"I know you were in the Freezer. Nearly as long as I. Do you find now that you're free, that you're somewhat out of sync?" Chesterton rubbed at his knee. "I don't feel that I quite fit in anymore. I'm out of step and I can never get back. Some kind of severe temporal dislocation. Have you experienced that?"

"Yeah, some. It's supposed to go away, fade eventually."

"I really don't believe, in my case at any rate, that it will." Chesterton studied him for a few seconds, nodding to himself. "Are you part of a major raid on our hideaway?"

"Not exactly."

"That's another odd thing. I can't seem to shake the notion that everything is going to go smash. I'll be found out, you know, and taken back up there. Did you dream while you were in the Freezer?"

"Yeah."

"They say, several of my learned colleagues, that one doesn't. But I know I did." He made a sad sighing sound. "I dreamed about my wife. Dreamed of scenes I'd never actually witnessed. Saw her, over and over in those long, terrible dreams, making love to others. The terrible thing is, you can't simply scream and wake up. Not in the Freezer. Each dream simply runs on and on. No way of knowing how long some of them lasted. All the men she'd been with. There were a lot of them."

"Sonny and Tora didn't force you to create a new supply of your virus, did they?" Jake said. "You did all this willingly."

"Yes, that's right," admitted Dr. Chesterton. "When I awakened here in Kyoto, it was explained to me what was wanted. A lovely city, by the way. Very peaceful. The Hokoris had brought me back to life in order that I might provide them with a sufficient supply of my XP-203 for their purposes. That was the price. If I refused, they had other names on their list."

"That didn't bother you—their purposes?"

"Not especially, Cardigan." Chesterton laughed a thin laugh. "I had, afterall, spent years doing the same sort of work for our government. Now I simply have a different employer."

"Several thousand people may die in San Francisco."

"Yes, that's how my synthetic virus works. Damn efficient stuff," he said. "Fifty years up in the Freezer is a long time. This, I assure you, is much better than—"

"You're helping to kill people."

"I always have, Cardigan. That's been my job. What you're actually objecting to is simply that the targets have changed."

Jake said evenly, "What I need from you is—"

"Am I correct in thinking your wife is like mine was?"

"I don't know."

"What I mean is, your wife made a cuckold of you. Very oldfashioned word. It hurts, though. That's basically why I killed her."

"The antidote to—"

"How do you feel about your wife's unfaithfulness?"

Jake moved nearer to him. "What I want is a copy of your research notes and whatever supply of the antidote you've got stockpiled here."

"Do you know how the virus is transmitted initially?"

"I imagine it's airborne, spread in some sort of mist form."

"That's exactly right," said the doctor. "Very easy to disseminate. In the field they've been using sprayguns about this size." He held his bony hands about three feet apart. "But, just for fun, I've also developed a compact spray unit for my own use." From a pocket of his smock he drew a small black pistol.

．

Muttering, feet dragging, the heavyset Japanese carried the wicker chair over to where Beth stood. He slammed it down, shoving it toward her and causing its legs to scrape harshly on the stone floor of the chill temple. "We should have killed this bitch long ago," he said, turning away and shuffling back to the vicinity of the huge golden Buddha.

"There are several reasons," said the tinny-sounding voice of Tora Hokori, "for allowing Miss Kittridge to remain alive."

Beth rested a hand on the back of the chair, but didn't sit in it. "I'm not, I have to tell you, especially in a mood to help you," she said in the direction of the container that held Tora's brain.

"Let's simply kill her." The Japanese jerked a goldhandled lazgun from his shoulder holster.

"No, Dr. Hyaku. Please, put that silly gun away now."

"A personalized gun such as this is far from silly, my dear." The neobiologist scowled at Beth, then at the silver cylinder. Muttering, he jammed the handsome gun away inside his loose black jacket. "When my students presented it to me, the honor involved was quite significant."

"That was several years ago," reminded Tora. "Your reputation has dimmed considerably since then."

Hyaku said, "Obviously, Tora, or otherwise I wouldn't be working for you at such an insultingly low salary."

The voxbox rattled when Tora laughed. "Miss Kittridge, I'd appreciate your telling me what stage your father's anti-Tek work has reached."

"I really don't have much idea," answered Beth. "He and I don't see much of each other, and I no longer assist him."

"A shame. I feel that family ties are the most important ties one has in life," said Tora. "I continue to miss my brother, Sonny, a great deal. That's one of the reasons I've ordered certain people killed. Revenge."

"People such as Kurt Winterguild?"

"He was one. Jake Cardigan is another I intend to kill."

"Jake had nothing to do with your brother's—"

"Did you summon me to this dismal hole simply that I might witness this pointless debate?" asked Dr. Hyaku impatiently. "You no longer have a body, Tora, but I do. I can't tolerate the cold and damp around here."

"Shrines are often cold and damp," Tora told him. "We'll leave the question of your father's researches for now. You're also an expert in the area of robotics, aren't you, Miss Kittridge?"

"No more than the people you already have working for you."

"Nevertheless, I'd like you to examine this new body that they've fashioned for me."

"A waste of time," put in the doctor. "Your brain is never going to function inside that android, Tora. Accept the fact and let us get on with the—"

"What do you say, Miss Kittridge?"

"Installing a viable human brain into an android host body has been routinely done for years," she replied. "There's no reason why it shouldn't work for you."

"Buffoons," commented Dr. Hyaku. "She employs technicians who are essentially buffoons. Pays many of them more than she doles out to me."

"If you assist me," said Tora, "it might prolong your life."

"And what about Jake's life?"

"There's no hope for Jake Cardigan," said Tora's voice. "He will die."

" I of course have long since made myself immune to XP-203," explained Dr. Chesterton, turning the spraypistol toward Jake. "You, however, don't have that advantage."

Saying nothing, Jake suddenly dived sideways. At the same time he yanked out his stungun and fired.

The beam hit Chesterton in the side. He rose to his feet, shivering, teeth grinding. Both hands went snapping open, the pistol loaded with the plague spray dropped to the office floor.

The color washed out of his face, his skin turned a sooty white. Chesterton started chewing violently at his lower lip, making a raspy snarling noise. Blood and froth spilled out, smearing the twisted smile that was pulling his mouth wide.

He managed to press one splayed hand to his chest before he toppled. Chesterton fell against the black couch. He bounced off it, tumbled down to the grey carpeting.

Blood came foaming out between his torn lips. His entire body jerked, shuddered, then was still.

Jake, frowning, looked from the fallen man to the stungun in his hand. "Christ, what happened?"

He approached the fallen figure, knelt on one knee. As he'd guessed, Chesterton was dead.

He'd apparently had some kind of shock reaction to the stungun shot. That did happen, but rarely. Jake had heard of a few instances, but never witnessed one before.

"Damn it." He stood. Jake felt no sorrow for the deadman, but this could mean he'd lost any chance of getting the antidote for the plague.

■

Slightly crouched, alert, Gomez moved along the corridor in search of Jake. The aircirc system in this stretch of underground facility wasn't functioning exactly right and several of the ceiling ducts were producing low rattling sounds.

Gomez was carrying a small aluminum suitcase, recently borrowed. He stopped suddenly, shifted the case to his left hand and drew out his stungun.

A door up ahead had started to swing open.

Letting his breath sigh slowly out, he lowered the gun. *"Amigo,"* he said quietly.

"You better tell me you had better luck than I did." Jake came, empty-handed, out of Dr. Chesterton's office.

"I've done fairly well," admitted his partner, patting the silver suitcase. *"Y usted?"*

"Well, I found Chesterton," replied Jake, pointing at the closed door with a thumb. "When he tried to run a field test of XP-203 on me, I used my stungun. That set off some kind of negative reaction in him—he died."

Gomez shrugged. "Tora and company weren't forcing the guy to work for them, were they?"

"Nope, Chesterton was doing it willingly."

"No great loss then."

"Except we didn't get around to talking about the antidote. And I couldn't find a damn thing in his—"

"Aquí." Smiling broadly, Gomez held up the aluminum case. "By persuading a techbot to help the cause, I am now the proud owner of a handsomely printed copy of Doc Chesterton's basic notes on the plague, its cause and cure. Plus a sample of the virus

and, more importantly, the antidote as well. So we are free to scram."

"That's great, Sid," said Jake. "All we have to do now is locate Beth. She isn't being held down here. I found that out."

"Then she's probably over in the Juunigwatsu Temple," said Gomez. "Do you have any idea which of these tunnels might lead over there?"

"I do, yeah."

Giving a robot-like bow, Gomez suggested, "Let's take a tour of the temple then."

.

"*Nueve,*" said Gomez as he dragged the large disabled black robot to the side of the harshly lit stone tunnel.

"Ten," said Jake.

"*Sí, es verdad.* I keep forgetting to include that one you decked."

They continued on in silence for another quarter mile. Then up ahead loomed a large teakwood door.

Jake said, "This ought to be the temple itself coming up."

"*Cuidado,*" cautioned his partner.

Jake eased the door open a few inches. Chill air and deep shadows confronted him.

Then he heard the sound of someone being slapped.

"That's enough, Dr. Hyaku," warned a harsh, metallic voice.

"I'm growing tired of her flippant answers."

"Get away from her."

"It's okay, Tora. He doesn't have a very powerful—"

Another slap.

"That's Beth." Opening the door wider, Jake dived across the threshold.

"Take it easy." Gomez failed to catch hold of his arm.

Jake found himself in the shadows that surrounded an immense golden Buddha who squatted on a dark pedestal.

Drawing his stungun, Jake started working his way around the huge statue.

There in a milky circle of light were Beth and a thickset Japanese who held a glittering goldhandled lazgun. Beyond them stood an array of heavy medical equipment that Jake couldn't quite identify.

"Leave her alone," Jake shouted and started running toward the man with the gun.

Hyaku swung around, taking aim at Jake.

Grabbing hold of the back of the wicker chair, Beth swung it up hard.

Two of the legs smacked the doctor's gun arm. He yowled, the lazgun went flying from his fingers.

The gun climbed up to a height of about ten feet, spinning, wobbling, gleaming. Then it fell.

When it hit a long, deadwhite piece of equipment, the gun discharged and a beam of sizzling orange light came spurting out. The beam hit the cylinder that held Tora's brain, slicing deeply into it.

From out of the voxbox came a brief, terrible scream of pain.

The silvery cannister had been cut clean in half and its contents came slithering out. The sustaining fluid and the brain itself spilled out. The brain, quivering and flopping, slid across the tabletop, then fell down to the chill stone floor.

Dr. Hyaku cried, "She's dead. You've killed Tora!"

Catching him by the shoulder, Jake spun the man around and hit him twice on the chin.

The doctor lost consciousness, slipped and fell. He landed in the mess that was all that was left of Tora Hokori.

::42::

A thin afternoon fog was drifting in low across San Francisco Bay. The visitors' landing area next to the Marina Hospital was misty, too.

Jake leaned back in the seat of the aircar for a moment after they'd landed.

Beth touched his cheek with her fingertips. "You okay?"

"Huh?" He had been staring out at the swirling fog.

"We've arrived. I was assuming you knew that, since you were flying this thing."

Jake shook his head. "Yeah, sorry," he said. "My mind was wandering. That happens frequently with elderly fellows."

"Kate is going to be okay. You already know that."

"Sure, that wasn't what I was brooding about." He unhooked his safety gear, climbed out of the skycar into the fog.

"Dan then?" Beth joined him and took hold of his hand.

"I'm glad that I'm going to be looking after him until Kate's released. But picking Dan up today—I don't know. Makes me uneasy."

"It won't be as—"

"Jake, talk to us!"

They were coming across the foggy hospital lot toward him. Seven reporters, including Pachter of Newz, Inc., Gary Insatsu of the

Shinbun Vidnews Service, the big chromeplated robot from Time-Life Media, Ivey of the *SF Fax-Exam* and the silverhaired young woman Jake still couldn't place.

"You've saved Frisco," said the lanky Ivey, "so tell us how that feels."

"First," said Insatsu, "tell us how many people you killed in Japan in order to get your hands on the antidote."

"Folks," said Jake, slowly but not stopping, "the Cosmos Detective Agency issued a statement this morning down in GLA. That pretty much answers most of the—"

"It doesn't mention your partner's torrid romance with one of our ace reporters," said Pachter. "Give us the dirt on that, Jake."

"Forget it, Pach," advised the silverhaired reporter. "Jake, the National Disease Control Agency completed its tests on the antidote and has okayed its use. That means your wife's life will be saved, along with—"

"Right now," he cut in, "I'm just here to pick up my son. After I take care of that, maybe we can all have a chat." He increased his pace.

"About those killings in Kyoto," persisted Insatsu.

The silverhaired reporter inquired, "How do you think your wife will react to your relationship with Miss Kittridge when she comes out of her coma and—yow!"

Beth had kicked her in the shin.

Breaking free of the reporters, Jake and Beth hurried into the hospital.

In the Reception Area Jake spotted the tall, thin Dr. Goedewaagen, who was the director of the Isolation Wing. "Doctor, I'm here to take charge of my son. He's being released today."

"I don't quite understand, Mr. Cardigan. Was there something wrong over in Observation?"

Jake frowned. "Observation? We just arrived."

"But I talked to you right here less than ten minutes ago. I personally handed you the necessary release papers for your son and thanked you for—"

"Jesus, a kamikaze." Letting go of Beth, Jake started running toward the ramp.

■

According to the glosigns on the walls and the arrows on the floor, Jake had only one more ramp to go and then he'd be in the Observation Wing.

It had taken him at least five minutes to get this far. That meant the android dupe now might have as much as a fifteen-minute lead.

A part of him was braced, waiting to hear the horrible sound that would mean the kamikaze had made contact with his son.

"Damn Tora," he growled as he ran, dodging startled human nurses and oblivious white enameled medibots.

Jake knew he should have realized they were going to try this. Dr. Chesterton told him about all the pictures of him Tora had collected. Pictures to use in constructing a believable andy simulacrum. A sim filled with explosives, programmed to recognize Dan and to detonate the moment he touched it.

Each breath Jake took burned his lungs, and his legs were starting to ache.

"No time," he said to himself. "Not enough time to get to Dan."

Jake pushed himself to go faster, ignoring the pain.

Two swing doors ahead labeled OBSERVATION.

He pushed through and was in a large rooftop area. There was a plastiglass dome over the Reception Room and the foggy afternoon showed outside. Around the oval room ran a bright yellow ramp that was dotted with white benches. A few patients were scattered around on them.

And standing by an empty bench all the way across the big room was Jake Cardigan.

A damn convincing facsimile.

He was smiling, holding out his arms.

Not more than a hundred yards away was Dan, carrying a small tan suitcase and accompanied by the nurse who'd befriended him. The nurse stopped, patted him on the shoulder. Dan started alone toward the waiting kamikaze.

"Dan! Get back!" shouted Jake, running along the ramp.

His son, surprised, stopped still and stared at him.

The simulacrum, though, started moving. "Danny," it said, "you know me."

"Down, get down!" warned Jake, running for all he was worth.

He caught up with the kamikaze, hit it hard with his shoulder.

The android staggered, went tottering into the plastiglass wall. A panel shattered and the simulacrum fell out into the mist. It was still about fifty feet from the ground when it exploded with an immense thundering boom.

Jake turned away from the misty afternoon.

Dan came slowly up to him, a smile growing on his pale face. "You saved my life," he said quietly, dropping his suitcase to the ramp. Then he jumped forward and put both arms around his father, hugging tight. "I love you."

Jake returned the hug. He smiled.